Mistletoe and Wine

Denise Devine

USA Today Bestselling Author

A Sweet Small Town Christmas Romance

Wild Prairie Rose Books

Mistletoe and Wine

Print Edition

https://www.deniseannettedevine.com

Neither ghostwriters nor artificial intelligence were used in the creation of this book. This entire story is the original work of Denise Devine.

ISBN: 978-1-943124-49-7

Published in the United States of America

Wild Prairie Rose Books

Edited by L. Ness and A. Speed

Cover Design by Raine English

Mistletoe and Wine

The holiday decorations are up but business is down. Is it really the most wonderful time of the year?

Allyson Cramer is determined to keep The Ramblin' Rose afloat. If the bar closes, her employees will lose their jobs, and she'll default on her loan. Despite her hard work, the situation becomes critical when the new manager of the pool hall lures her best customers away. Adding insult to injury, Max drops in one day to be "neighborly," bearing gifts and inviting her to lunch. The last thing she wants is to humor a competitor, but this handsome, gregarious man piques her curiosity. Will she gain the secret to his success or lose her heart to him instead?

Ho-ho-ho, Max Reardon needs a change of scenery—and fast.

His reputation and his job are destroyed when his boss' drunken wife, Sybil, brazenly makes a pass at him in public and wants to become friends with benefits. Disgusted, Max retreats to West Loon Bay to spend the holidays managing his uncle's pool hall and to contemplate his future. He doesn't plan to stay. The trouble is, the moment he meets Allyson, he's drawn to her. They share a kiss under the mistletoe and now he can't stop thinking about her. Unfortunately, he soon learns that Sybil won't stop thinking about *him.* And that's when his problems *really* begin.

Get your copy today! You'll fall in love with the people of West Loon Bay.

Let's keep in touch!

Sign up for ***Denise's Diary***, my monthly newsletter at:

https://www.deniseannettedevine.com/newsletter

You'll be the first to know about new releases, sales and special events.

Chapter One

November 1st

West Loon Bay, Minnesota

Multi-colored twinkle lights, pine garland twisted with scarlet berry clusters, and red velvet bows lined the large front windows of The Ramblin' Rose bar. A seven-foot tree laden with brightly colored ornaments and strings of glowing lights hugged one corner of the dance floor while Vince Gill's angelic voice filled the air with a classic Christmas song.

The warmth and nostalgia of the season should have filled her with joy, but instead, Allyson Cramer struggled to get into the holiday mood. She sighed, preoccupied with the dismal state of the bar's finances as she taped a string of mini-Christmas lights to the shelving on the wall behind the bar.

Across the room, Ashton Wyatt pinned a collage of handmade paper snowflakes frosted with white glitter on the wall. "I don't know why we're bothering to decorate," she complained in a gloomy voice as she pivoted away from the decorations and twisted her silky brown hair into a thick ponytail. Ashton and her younger sister, Grace, were Allyson's cousins and co-owners of the bar. "If things keep going the way they are," Ashton said, "we probably won't even be in business by Christmas."

"It's not our fault business is down," Allyson argued as she let go of the lights and spun around. The tape suddenly gave way, and the lights fell to the floor. She stared in annoyance at the heap of green wire at her feet. "Tourist season is over. People have pulled in their docks and closed up their cabins until next summer."

West Loon Bay resided on the south shore of Lake Tremolo, a large body of water encircled by fifty miles of shoreline and thick, old-growth forests. Ranking in the top five percent of the largest lakes in Minnesota, it was famous for its superb walleye population, modern boat facilities, and beautiful resorts.

"We weren't slow in November last year," Ashton persisted. She turned to her sister. "Were we, Grace?"

Grace, the youngest of the trio, flipped her long, thick braid of dark hair over her shoulder as she placed a small silk poinsettia plant next to the cinnamon-scented candle on each table. She wore skinny jeans, and a black T-shirt embellished with a red metallic rose, their company uniform. "No," she said quietly, "but we had just opened for business and people were curious."

Wiping her hands on her apron, Grace approached the bar. "What are we going to do, Allyson? If things don't get better, we'll have to close. Our employees will all be out of a job." She winced, her large brown eyes reflecting worry. "What a terrible thing to do to them just before Christmas!"

"I don't know," Allyson replied, reaching down to scoop up the lights, "but whatever we decide, we need to get going on it immediately."

"Mom heard some gossip at Trudi's beauty salon when she was getting her hair done that Uncle Wally might be closing down the pool hall for a couple of months," Ashton announced as she slid onto a bar stool. "His knees are getting so bad that he can barely walk. Mom says he has to go to a rehab facility for a couple of months after he gets the first one replaced so the pool hall may be closed until he comes home.

We could get some new business from the closure, at least for a while."

Grace made a face, demonstrating her displeasure at the prospect of luring customers from Uncle Wally's billiard room. "*E-w-w-w*. That place is gross. All the guys who hang out there are too. Uncle Wally lets them swear, make sexist jokes, and belch out loud at both ends!"

Ashton snickered at Grace's cringe-worthy word picture. "Now you know why the worst guys in town like that place so much. They can be themselves, and no one cares!"

Uncle Wally wasn't the girls' uncle. He wasn't related to anyone in town, for that matter, but everyone called him that, just the same. Decades ago, he'd come to West Loon Bay to teach high school geography and coach the football team. After his wife died of cancer, he retired from teaching, sold his farm, and bought the pool hall. His rotund belly and neatly trimmed beard made him the perfect Santa at Christmastime. He never had kids of his own, but if he encountered children from his former students, he always dug into his pockets for coins to give them. Over time, the name "Uncle Wally" became his identity.

"Business isn't as bad as it seems," Allyson said, desperate to convince not only the Wyatt sisters but herself as well. "Our income is enough to keep us afloat for now if nothing else goes wrong. It's not our fault that we've had so many equipment breakdowns this year."

So far, the water heater had needed replacement, the walk-in cooler required extensive repairs when it stopped cooling, spoiling all the food stored in it, and they also had to buy a new ice maker. They'd covered the costs, but the expenses had nearly depleted their bank account. Thank goodness they had saved last year's holiday decorations to use again this year.

"The three of us work our tails off and yet after we cover the payroll for our employees, we're only making minimum wage," Ashton said, frowning as she leaned her elbows on the bar. "I'm sick of working for peanuts."

Allyson dropped the light string in a pile on the counter, giving up on it for now. Instead, she scooped ice into a frosted mug, grabbed the soda gun, and filled the mug with Coke, Ashton's favorite drink. "We've had some setbacks, but we'll get there." She put a straw in the mug and shoved the fizzy concoction toward Ashton, desperate to convince not only her cousins that they would prevail, but herself as well. "With the holidays coming up, we'll draw downtown shoppers with our lunch and dinner specials and entice people to stop in on their way home from work with cheap happy hour appetizers. More customers will result in more tips so that will supplement our pay."

"Well, we must do *something*, and fast," Ashton argued as she twirled the straw in her drink. "If things don't get better soon, I'll have to start looking for a new job. You guys will too."

Allyson exchanged horrified glances with Grace.

Grace turned to her sister. "You're giving up already? What happened to the agreement we made to work together to make this place a success?"

Stunned by Ashton's announcement, Allyson placed her palms on the edge of the bar to steady herself. "What about the startup loan we got from Aunt Rose? How will we pay her back if we simply give up and shut the place down? She put her heart and soul into The Ramblin' Rose for twenty-five years. Now it's our turn. We can't quit."

The startup loan had meant a lot to Allyson. Her mother, Ruth, and Aunt Rose were twin sisters and she'd always been Rose's favorite niece. She couldn't let her aunt down by defaulting on the loan.

Ashton stared at her Coke, her cheeks flushing with anger at finding herself outnumbered by her sister and her cousin. "It's better than going down with the ship."

"Oh, so now you're comparing The Ramblin' Rose to the

Titanic?" Incensed, Allyson slapped a bar towel on the counter. "That's not being very supportive!"

"Hey!" Ashton sat back and folded her arms. "At least I'm being realistic!"

"Hang on, you guys." Grace raised her palms in a peacemaking gesture. "Stop arguing, okay? We need to increase revenue, but we're not bankrupt yet." She stared at Ashton. "So, before you decide to bail on us, at least give the business one more chance. I say we meet here tomorrow morning and work on a strategy to bring in more customers." She glanced from her sister to her cousin. "Does that sound reasonable?"

Tense from arguing, Allyson's fingers clenched the bar as she anxiously waited for Ashton's answer.

"Fine," Ashton replied reluctantly. "I'll stick it out for now, but if we don't start making some decent money soon, I'm done working my tail off for this place."

Allyson sighed with relief. She'd avoided shuttering the place for now. The trouble was, staying open amounted to only a small victory. The real battle was in *keeping* the bar open and that meant coming up with a plan that was nothing short of a miracle.

I can't fail at this, she thought desperately. *I've already failed at one business, but this time it's worse. This time I'll be letting down Aunt Rose. She believes in me. She wouldn't have offered me an interest-free startup loan otherwise.*

Not only that, but Allyson still had an outstanding bill to cover from the demise of her first business adventure—her ill-fated interior design company. The company wasn't the problem. From the get-go, their business had grown by leaps and bounds. No, it was her partner, Janeen, who'd destroyed both of their reputations and their credit when she absconded with the money in their account, leaving thousands of dollars of unpaid bills on the table.

The bankruptcy court took care of their creditors, but Allyson vowed to Sawyer Daniels that she'd personally pay him the ten thousand dollars the bankruptcy had wiped out for the remodeling work he'd done for her company. She had no choice. Not only was Sawyer her best friend from childhood, but he was now Ashton's newlywed husband as well. She'd promised him the money would come from her profits from The Ramblin' Rose—and she meant it.

Andy Williams' mellow voice suddenly crooned, "It's the most wonderful time of the year…"

Was it? Being broke at Christmas didn't rate high on her list of "a few of my favorite things." She never thought that at twenty-nine years old she'd find herself on the verge of going bankrupt for the second time in her life, but sadly, it was a very real possibility.

She had to come up with a plan to save her business—and fast—but she was so stressed out by the prospect of going belly-up again *before Christmas* that she couldn't concentrate long enough to compose a list of ideas much less think rationally about her future.

Determination, desperation, and a stubborn streak were all she had. It had to be enough.

Chapter Two

November 2nd

Downtown Minneapolis, Minnesota

Max Reardon leaned against the edge of his desk with his cell phone to his ear, struggling to find a nice way to give the caller a firm *no*.

"It's not possible, Mom," he argued gently as he pushed himself away from his desk and paced his office at the Skyview Fitness Center and Spa. "I'm sorry, but I don't have enough vacation time to take over Uncle Wally's business while he's recovering, and I can't take a leave of absence for that long. We're short-staffed in the gym right now. Besides, there's a good chance I'm going to get a promotion."

He stopped in front of the large window in his office and gazed at the glow of multi-colored Christmas lights illuminating the nighttime sky across downtown Minneapolis. "My boss, Leo Lawrence, is going to promote someone on his management team to general manager so he can semi-retire and I'm on the shortlist. He's announcing his decision this week."

"That's wonderful, Max," Peggy Reardon replied in a soft, feminine voice. "You've been working at that fancy gym now for a long time and I know you've done a great job. It's about time they offered you a big promotion. You deserve it!"

"Thanks, Mom, but it's more than a gym. It's a luxury fitness center," he said evenly, surprised that she'd never really understood the difference. "Skyview has state-of-the-art equipment, including a spa with sauna and massage facilities. We also have yoga classes and a health bar. If I get the promotion, I'll be in charge over all of that."

Five years ago, Leo hired him as a personal trainer. After a couple of years, Max advanced to assistant manager of the gym and eventually became the manager. He liked his present job, but he knew it so well that lately he'd become bored with it and needed something more. Something challenging.

"I just wish I could find someone to take over the pool hall for Wally," Peggy said with a sigh. "He desperately needs a knee operation and I'm worried that if he can't find someone to manage the pool hall in his absence, he'll cancel the appointment. You know how stubborn my brother is!"

Max stared at the floor, wishing he could tactfully end this conversation. He had nothing in common with his Uncle Wally's pool hall, but most of all, he hated the idea of spending time in West Loon Bay, that dinky tourist town way out in the sticks. He'd spent enough summers there at Uncle Wally's farm back when he was a kid—bored to death. Weeding carrots and collecting eggs didn't compare with riding his bike to the park with his friends.

When Uncle Wally's wife, Dorothy died, he sold the farm and moved into town, guaranteeing that Max would never have to visit that place again. That is until today…

"Doesn't he have an assistant manager or a friend in town who could babysit his pool hall while he's gone? It's not a huge operation."

"He does," Peggy replied in a worried tone, "but the boy isn't mature enough to oversee the business on his own and frankly, Wally doesn't trust anyone else to manage the place."

The sharp clickety-clack of a woman's heels on the stone floor outside his office gave him the excuse he needed to say goodbye. Inhaling a deep breath of relief, he told his mother he had to go and disconnected the call just as Leo Lawrence's wife rounded the corner wearing a skin-tight dress in red satin and four-inch heels. The short, dark-haired beauty had thick shoulder-length curls and full red lips. A teardrop-shaped diamond pendant glittered in the light, nestled in the fold of her ample cleavage.

"We missed you at happy hour. Where were you?" she said in a tight voice, her disappointment palpable. She leaned against the door frame, steadying herself as though she'd consumed a few cocktails too many. "All of the other managers were there to celebrate my birthday. You're the only one who didn't show up."

No one knew her exact age, but if the gossip floating around the fitness center was true, Sybil had just turned fifty-six, which made her ten years younger than Leo.

"I had some paperwork to finish," Max said in a serious tone as he placed his cell phone on his desk. "I'm sorry. I lost track of the time." He wanted to be caught up and well-organized so that if he did get the promotion, he could step into the general manager slot immediately.

"You're forgiven—this time." She held up a bottle of champagne and two flutes, treating him to a confident smile. "So, I'm bringing the party to you." She walked toward him; her gaze locked onto his with the force of a tractor beam. "Besides, there's something we need to discuss. In private."

Max's chest tightened. The last thing he wanted was to get on the bad side of Sybil and risk offending her, but he *really* didn't want to polish off an entire bottle of bubbly with his boss' wife behind closed doors and generate a fresh supply of gossip. Especially in her present condition. She'd obviously already had enough.

Deliberately leaving the door open, he gestured toward a pair of padded chairs positioned in front of his desk. "All right. Have a seat."

“That won’t be necessary.” She stopped so close to him that they were almost touching. The powerful floral signature of her French rose perfume filled his nostrils, making it difficult to concentrate. “I believe in *interactive* conversation.” She set the flutes on his desk and shoved the bottle toward him. “Open this so we can celebrate properly.”

He glanced at the bottle but made no move to accept it. Sybil King had a drinking problem, an ego problem, a penchant for younger men, and wore fashions that exposed more skin than a nudist colony. Rumors of her unfaithfulness to Leo had been circulating among the fitness center staff for years. He didn’t know if the gossip held any truth or not, but he had no interest in finding out. “Aren’t you supposed to meet Leo for dinner? He told me earlier that he’d made reservations at your favorite seafood restaurant.”

She waved the suggestion away. “You mean, me, Leo, and his professional babysitters. I’m in no hurry to have his stupid henchmen looking over my shoulder all night. I want to have a drink with you first.” She followed up with a sly grin as she shoved the bottle toward him again. “We both have something to celebrate.”

Max blinked, blindsided by her remark. *What?* Once the hint in her answer sunk in, he froze with his fingers absently wrapped around the neck of the bottle. “Has Leo made a decision? Are you telling me that I’m getting the general manager position?”

She moved closer, toying with a button on his shirt. “Well, not yet, but that’s only because I haven’t made my preference known first.” She laughed triumphantly at his confusion. “My money financed this operation too. Unfortunately for Leo, I hold fifty-one percent. He won’t admit this to a soul, but when it comes to the business end of our relationship, my dear husband does *not* hold all the cards. *I* do.” Sliding her palms slowly upward on Max’s broad, muscular chest, she stared up into his eyes with a beguiling smile. “And I choose *you*.”

Her message came through loud and clear catching him off guard.

His palms began to sweat, and he nearly dropped the bottle on her foot. With a shaky hand, he placed the champagne bottle on his desk and slowly pulled her manicured hands away. The job he'd applied for didn't include sleeping with the boss' wife, and he had no desire to add stud service to Sybil King to his job description under 'other duties as assigned.'

"Not going to happen Sybil. I want the job, but not that bad," Max said gravely as he dropped her hands and stepped back, putting some much-needed distance between them. "I respect Leo. I won't betray him like that."

Sybil glared at him, her beautiful dark eyes flaring at his defiance. "Betray him? Leo is no Boy Scout! He's cheated on me more times than I can count. The only reason we stay together is because our money and investments are so tangled together that it would be a legal nightmare to get divorced."

She lurched forward and placed her palms on his chest again. "Look, it isn't what you think," she implored, her eyes softening. "This has nothing to do with Leo. It's the chemistry between you and me, Max. Don't deny it."

He slid his fingers around her wrists to peel them off his chest. "I don't mess around with married women, Sybil. The fact that you're not listening to me shows you've had too much to drink and you're not thinking straight. Let's talk about the job tomorrow when you're sober."

She pulled away and raised her hand to slap him, but his large palm engulfed her slender one before it could connect with his cheek. "How dare you accuse me of being too drunk to know what I'm doing!" She lifted her chin high. "I'm not too drunk to fire you for insulting me!"

He backed away and grabbed his cell phone off the desk. It was time to leave before people in the gym heard her shouting and came to see what all the fuss was about. "I'm not trying to insult you. What you want me to do is an insult to your husband." He pointed a thumb at his chest. "My boss. A man who happens to be as jealous as he is rich. The idea is crazy!"

"I'm crazy for you, Max!"

He'd learned a long time ago to separate his personal life from his professional employment. The job of personal trainer brought him into close physical contact with many female clients. Some of those women were very beautiful. Some were downright irresistible. And married. Due to the advice of a wise friend who had at one time been *his* trainer, he'd never allowed himself to be blinded by his desires and succumb to temptation. Over the years, that principle had served him well and it would be the right choice again now.

"Look, you're being unreasonable," he said as he shoved his phone into his back pocket and checked his front pocket to make sure he had his car key. "I'm not going to be a pawn in your marital game of tit-for-tat. I don't want the job if sleeping with you is what you expect me to do to get it."

Before he had a chance to walk past her, Sybil grabbed the front of his shirt and pulled him toward her, jamming her full mouth against his. Her arms locked around his neck like an octopus as she kissed him, pulling him deep into an embrace but her boldness didn't generate the effect on him that he knew she'd expected. Placing his hands on her waist, he angrily pushed her away. What kind of game was she playing? It didn't matter—he didn't want to play along, and he suddenly realized how a woman must feel when a man put her in this position.

"Max, I've got the…the schedules you…you…"

Shocked to hear another voice, Max looked up. The stout female wearing a black pantsuit and matching, black-framed glasses stopped in the doorway and gasped. The heavy folders containing the employee schedules clattered to the floor. Before he could say anything, Susan Jeffers turned and bolted from the room.

Judging by her reaction, Susan had witnessed the exchange

between him and Sybil. Within minutes, everyone would know what had happened. His reputation was shot now with no way to repair it. No way could he explain to Leo what happened without laying all the blame on Sybil and making it look like he was trying to frame her. Sadly, five years of hard work just went down the drain. Not only that, but he couldn't use this job now as a reference to find another one.

Angry, he shoved Sybil out of the way, grabbed his sports jacket off the coat tree, and stormed out.

"Where are you going? Don't you dare walk out on me, Max. I order you to come back here!" Sybil cried after him.

He stopped and looked back at the woman who'd just screwed up his life. "I don't take orders from you any longer."

"Look, if you're worried about Susan, I'll talk to her," she said breathlessly. "I'll explain what happened. She'll be more than happy to keep quiet in exchange for a nice Christmas bonus."

He didn't care if she promised Susan a slice of the company to buy her silence. It wasn't his problem. "It doesn't matter to me. I'm done here." Slinging his sports jacket over his shoulder, he walked out, never looking back.

He took the back stairs down to the parking garage, ten floors below hoping to work off some of his anger in the process. Going through the heated garage, he slipped his arms into his jacket as he walked toward his car mulling over Sybil's actions.

She'd always been friendly with him, but he'd never given her any encouragement or led her on to believe that he wanted more from her. He'd always treated her with respect. So why did she go over the line tonight? And when Susan came upon them, why didn't it embarrass Sybil? It didn't make sense.

Shrugging off his thoughts, he pulled out his phone and called his mother. Peggy answered on the second ring. "Hello, Mom? It's me, Max.

Yeah, say, I've been thinking about what you said. About Uncle Wally needing my help? I've decided that I probably should take over managing the pool hall so he can get his knee fixed. It's important that he gets the care he needs. Besides, I need a change of scenery for a while…"

He hadn't changed his dislike of small-town life, but spending time in West Loon Bay would give him some down time to clear his head and think about his future.

At the same time, he wanted to be where no one would think of looking if they tried to find him. Especially Sybil King.

Chapter Three

November 15th

Christmas music echoed throughout the cavernous room as Allyson wiped down the counters after the last lunch customer left, disappointed that their new push to bring in more business hadn't increased their customer base. This week had been the slowest yet. Elvis' Blue Christmas suddenly came on, dropping her morale to rock bottom. Grimacing at the lousy timing of the song, she reached over to the sound system control unit and turned the volume down.

"I'm making some onion rings for us," Grace said through the large serving window as the air filled with the snap, crackle, and pop sounds of beer-battered onion rings being lowered into the deep fryer. Today, she wore her thick dark braid twisted into a large bun and secured it with decorative Japanese wooden hair sticks decorated with tiny Christmas bells. They jingled every time she moved her head. "Allyson, why don't you pour a couple of fresh Cokes for us? We need a break."

"Yeah," Ashton said as she pulled the stretchy ponytail holder out of her long, silky brown hair. "We need a break from boredom."

During the afternoon lull before the happy hour crowd began filing in, the girls usually took turns helping Mrs. Olson with food prep, but their business had been so slow that there wasn't much to do. Except munch on junk food.

"It's only been two weeks," Allyson argued as she leaned against the bar. "Our next happy hour ad comes out in the Bay News tomorrow. We should see an uptick by the end of this week."

"I hope so," Grace replied softly and pulled down a red plastic burger basket, lining it with a precut sheet of white waxed paper. "We need the money. This place is like a funeral parlor in the afternoon."

"I've got an idea." Ashton grabbed Allyson's wet towel off the bar and walked toward a table in the dining area. "Why don't we dress up in costumes?" She looked down at her black jeans, black Ramblin' Rose T-shirt and tennis shoes. "It would be an improvement over this grubby look."

Allyson grabbed three frosted mugs from the chest freezer and set them on the counter, unsure about Ashton's brainy *idea.* "You mean like Christmas characters?"

"Yeah," Ashton replied, vigorously wiping down the chairs at their favorite table. "I'm thinking we could be characters from Santa's workshop or something like that."

Allyson frowned. She grabbed a metal scoop and began filling the mugs with ice cubes. "Sorry, but we're fresh out of elf costumes. Besides, who's going to be Mrs. Santa?" She and Ashton turned in unison to stare at Grace.

"Oh, no you don't," Grace grumbled as she shook her head, her large brown eyes widening at the mention of such a thing. "Not me. Nada!"

Allyson laughed. "Oh, but you're short like Mrs. Claus and you'd look so cute in those wire-rimmed glasses!"

Laughing, Grace grabbed a slice of tomato, stepped into the doorway, and threw it at her.

As soon as the appetizer was ready to eat, they sat at their employee table, the one closest to the kitchen, munching on crispy, hot onion rings dipped in ketchup.

"Uncle Wally went to St. Paul to have his knee operation, and his nephew is now managing the pool hall," Grace said as she pulled a hot onion ring out of the basket and dropped it on her plate.

Allyson rolled her eyes at the mention of West Loon Bay's worst establishment.

Ashton snorted. "I feel sorry for him."

Grace swirled the onion ring in a puddle of ketchup. "Mom says the nephew's a total hunk. He's the talk of the town. All the ladies in her book club have been dropping by the pool hall for lunch just to get a good look at him. He's got a body like Duane Johnson and Arnold Schwarzenegger. You know, chiseled abs, and a sexy tan."

Allyson dropped her onion ring and gasped. "Aunt Robin said *that*?"

Grace shrugged. "She was only repeating what the gals down at Trudi's beauty salon said. I guess they can't talk about anything else. It's gotten so bad that someone brought in a jar of smelling salts just in case the guy comes in to buy a bottle of men's shampoo."

"Oh, brother…" Allyson said and almost choked on her Coke. The sudden fizz in her nostrils brought tears to her eyes but even so, she couldn't help laughing. "I've heard everything now."

"Not yet," Grace countered. "Ricky Palmer stopped by the kitchen this morning to borrow some spices. He said that his new boss might drop in sometime to introduce himself to us."

"Why?" Ashton asked with a smirk. "Is he so desperate to get out of that pigsty that he's looking for a new job? A guy with his muscles would make a great dishwasher."

Their laughter abruptly ceased at the ringing of the phone. Grace jumped up to answer it behind the bar. "Ramblin' Rose, Grace speaking." She listened for a while, nodding and murmuring "hmmm..." to the caller's words as she licked ketchup off her fingers. "Okay, thanks for letting us know." She hung up the phone. "Speak of the devil, that was Ricky. He says his boss is on his way over here. Right now."

Allyson stood as the glass doors at the entrance suddenly flew open and a tall, broad-shouldered man wearing black Nike workout pants and a black polo shirt stood in the doorway holding a cardboard cup holder containing three Styrofoam coffee cups. Uncle Wally's chunky and arthritic golden lab, Sandy, followed at his heels, huffing from the block-long walk.

The door shut behind them, but not before a chilly breeze coming off Lake Tremolo seeped through, filling the room with crisp November air. The man didn't seem to notice.

Shivering, Allyson crossed her arms. So, this *hunk* of a guy was Uncle Wally's nephew? Holy mackerel, he sure didn't take after his uncle's side of the family. At. All. Uncle Wally stood about five feet six inches tall and was almost as round at the waist. This guy had a trim waist and solid, muscular arms that strained against the short sleeves of his shirt. She measured over six feet in four-inch heels, but this guy towered over her. He nearly bumped his head coming through the door. His thick, dark hair and closely cropped beard enhanced his image of a tough, confident man. His green eyes studied them with curiosity.

He strode toward Allyson in long, confident strides, his gaze never leaving hers, but seemingly taking in every inch of her person at the same time.

Whoa, mister, she thought indignantly. *I may run a honkey tonk, but I'm no barfly. Quit looking at me like I'm going to be your next conquest. You should be so lucky!*

Grace and Ashton stood next to her, too stunned to speak.

"Sandy, sit," he commanded softly to the dog. Sandy silently obeyed while watching his handler intently. Only seeing-eye dogs and emotional support animals were allowed in the bar, but Allyson refrained from mentioning it. Uncle Wally's dog probably needed therapy himself after living in the pool hall for most of his life.

"Good afternoon, ladies," the man said in a deep, sexy voice. "I'm Max Reardon, Wally Knudsen's nephew. I'm minding the store for him while he's taking care of some business in St. Paul."

Ashton and Grace stood mute, staring at him in awe.

"It's nice to meet you, Max," Allyson said quickly, embarrassed by the schoolgirl reaction of her coworkers. "I'm Allyson Cramer and these are my cousins." She gestured toward them one at a time. "Grace Wyatt and Ashton Wyatt-Daniels. We're co-managers of The Ramblin' Rose. Are you staying here temporarily while Uncle Wally is away or is West Loon Bay now your home?"

"It's great to meet you, too." He smiled, his lean, tanned face reflecting a man in his mid-thirties. "When my uncle returns, I'll be moving back home to Minneapolis. Small-town life," he said with a shrug, "is not my thing."

He stepped closer and held out the cup holder. "In the meantime, I brought you all a little something from the pool hall to warm you up on such a dark and chilly day. Pumpkin spice latte."

Though no one spoke right away, Allyson sensed a sudden resistance radiating off the girls like a tidal wave. Nothing wrong with a pumpkin spice latte…nothing at all. But from Uncle Wally's pool hall? That place was dirtier and smellier than her cat's litter box after eating seafood.

Ashton found her voice first. "Since when did Uncle Wally start serving lattes?" She stared worriedly at the cups as though they had been flavored with arsenic. "I thought his specialty was Budweiser."

Max pulled the first cup from the holder, offering it to Allyson. "The coffee machine is mine. I brought it with me because I need my double espresso in the morning. It's a pretty cool gizmo that also makes coffee, cappuccino, and of course, latte. We're offering specialty coffee now in the pool hall." He pushed the cup into Allyson's hand. "Thanks for giving Ricky the proper spices to make them. I kind of guessed the amount needed. I think it's fine, but you be the judge."

"Oh—okay," Allyson said and gingerly accepted the latte. His love for good coffee surprised her. She wondered how well specialty coffee would sell. Not many guys in this town had even tried an espresso much less preferred it over the weak, "old sock" tasting stuff most people served in West Loon Bay.

The exchange only lasted a moment, but as he handed off the cup to her, the brush of his fingers against hers caused a small earthquake of flutters to overtake her stomach—an awareness she hadn't sensed in a long time. Startled, she swallowed hard and glanced around, wondering if anyone had noticed it besides her. Grace and Ashton were so busy being mesmerized by their handsome visitor they didn't have a clue. West Loon Bay's tornado siren could go off and they wouldn't notice!

Max offered the remaining cups to the sisters and each girl hesitantly accepted his gift. Allyson waited apprehensively as the girls stared at each other, silently daring one another to brave the first taste.

Oh well, she thought as she pulled the plastic cover off hers and took a cautious sip. *If I die, I die. It's been so long since I've had a pumpkin spice latte, I'll take a chance...*

"Oh," she said with a groan as a mix of cinnamon, nutmeg, clove, steamed milk, and espresso, topped with whipped cream and pumpkin pie spice slid down her throat.

"What's wrong?" Grace cried.

Max frowned, looking worried. "Is it okay?"

"It's wonderful," Allyson whispered savoring the rich taste. "It's been so long since I've had one that I'd almost forgotten how much I love this stuff. Thank you."

Grace and Ashton tasted theirs, voicing their approval.

"Great," Max said enthusiastically while patting Uncle Wally's dog on the head. "The reason I came by is to extend an invitation to all of you to lunch tomorrow. Say, about two o'clock? Our lunch rush should be over by that time. My staff has been busy cleaning and making a lot of changes around the place, but the project is nearly done so I think it's time I got acquainted with the other business owners along Main Street."

Allyson nearly dropped her cup. "You—you want us to…what? Oh, no, we…we couldn't. We're too busy to leave the bar during the day."

Max made a point of glancing around. "Yeah, I can see that."

"Well, we've got food prep and…and…cleaning…and—"

"Can you smell that?" Grace blurted out. "I think something is burning." She set down her cup and grabbed Allyson by the arm. "We'll be right back!"

"Ow," Allyson complained in a muffled voice and jerked her arm away once they stood inside the kitchen. "Your fingernails pierce like tiger claws. What's going on with you?"

"We need to accept his invitation," Grace whispered.

Allyson stared at her in shock. "Are you crazy? That place is ptomaine central! We'll be lucky if we don't end up in the emergency room after eating there."

"Who says we have to eat anything? Let's just go down there and observe what's going on," Grace argued. "We need to find out what he's doing to get all of the ladies from Trudi's salon and Mom's book club to keep going there for lunch!"

Allyson scoffed. "That'll be the day. I'll never be that desperate."

Grace glared at her with a stubborn frown. "We *are* that desperate. We're going to the pool hall for lunch tomorrow and that's that!" She glanced toward the dining room hesitating. "And besides…I think he's kinda cute!"

"Grace!"

Grabbing Allyson by the arm again, Grace pulled her back into the bar. "False alarm," she said with an innocent smile. "It was just a piece of burnt toast that someone left on the counter. Max, we'd be delighted to accept your invitation to lunch."

Grace stared at both Allyson and her sister with a no-nonsense glare. "Right, girls?"

"Right!" Ashton chimed in and slurped her latte.

Allyson ripped her arm from Grace's grasp once more and stood to one side silently seething. *I am not going to lunch tomorrow at the pool hall and swallow my pride while his staff serves our old customers. It's humiliating!*

"All right. We have a date then," Max said as he and Sandy headed for the door. "I won't keep you any longer. I know you're…er…busy."

"Smart aleck," Allyson muttered silently to his back. And for the record, it was *not* a date. Just the same, she was a little curious. Okay, she was a lot curious. What was the secret of his success? She intended to find out.

Chapter Four

November 16th

Max walked through the pool hall, double-checking to make sure all the Christmas decorations had been hung, the booths were clean, and the condiments were full. The girls from The Ramblin' Rose were coming for lunch this afternoon and he wanted the place to be in tip-top shape. He didn't know what to expect yesterday when he'd visited their bar, but he found them to be exceptional women. Especially the tall, blonde one—Allyson Cramer. With her, however, everything about her seemed a contradiction to him. She was just too classy, too sharp to be content with slinging hash and hawking beers in a small-town honky-tonk for the rest of her life. The way she'd looked at him had stirred his curiosity and he couldn't stop thinking about her. She seemed curious about him too.

Let it go, he thought pessimistically to himself. *I didn't come here to find a girlfriend. I'm only sticking around until my uncle comes home. Anything beyond friendship with the women in this town is out of the question.*

"Maddie, put this in the ladies' room," he said to one of the servers as he handed the young lady a clear bud vase filled with two red roses, baby's breath, and a red velvet bow. He'd stopped by the grocery store on his way to work and picked up the arrangement from the tiny floral area next to the customer service desk.

One of the first things he'd undertaken as soon as he got a good look at the dismal state of his uncle's pool hall was to assign permanent cleaning duties to Uncle Wally's employees, including sanitizing the restrooms every night after closing. The pool hall had a reputation for being the dirtiest establishment in town, and from the looks of things, rightly so. Besides an abundance of dog hair, dirt, and dust, everything smelled like rancid grease and old cigarette smoke. His allergies went ballistic during his first day on the job, giving him a pounding headache, and he had vowed to do something about it.

Years of grime were scrubbed off the furniture and equipment including Sandy's private corner where he usually lounged on his soft dog bed. The storerooms were cleaned out, junk was thrown away. Then Max set about fixing broken equipment and painting every wall, every strip of woodwork in bold colors. Working long hours to get it done tired him out, but it also provided him with a way to keep his mind off the disastrous end to his career at the fitness center and the bleak outlook of his future job search. He needed something to distract him and the mess at the pool hall kept him super busy.

Ricky Palmer, his assistant manager, leaned toward the vase in Maddie's hand and sniffed the flowers. "Sure smells nice, Boss. Do you think stuff like this will bring more girls into the pool hall?"

Eddie Erikson, one of the regulars who came in every day, sat at the bar eating a double cheeseburger and fries for lunch. Tall and lanky, Eddie ate like a horse and never gained an ounce. His strawberry blond hair and reddish beard made him look younger than his twenty-nine years. Like most of the regulars, he wore a dark T-shirt and faded jeans. And he had a smart mouth.

Eddie picked up his half-pound cheeseburger with both hands and grinned at Ricky. "If it does, they ain't gonna be interested in a loser like you!"

Everyone sitting at the bar laughed.

Ricky gave the hecklers a dirty look but didn't respond. Turning his back on them, he trudged into the kitchen to check on a customer's food order.

Max watched the incident unfold with irritation. He kept his distance to allow Ricky to handle the situation himself, but it was obvious that Ricky lacked both the nerve and the maturity to stand up to the bullies who made fun of him whenever they could. Judging by the way he reacted, the heckling had probably been going on all his life.

From what Max had observed so far, Ricky Palmer was a good kid at heart, and he understood why his uncle had taken the twenty-three-year-old under his wing. Ricky had intelligence, common sense, and an abundance of creativity. He'd make a good business manager once he conquered his self-esteem issues. And that meant standing up to the town bullies.

The girls arrived at exactly two o'clock, cautiously glancing around as they walked into the pool hall.

"Oh, my goodness," Grace exclaimed with a gasp as she twirled around in black velvet leggings and a red plaid top layered with a black, knee-length sweater. "I can't believe what you've done to this place. It's amazing!"

"Yeah," Ashton chimed in wearing mahogany-colored jeans and an orange sweater. "It's actually clean and the dead animal smell is gone!"

The two guys sitting at the bar laughed.

Allyson cleared her throat and gave Ashton a quick nudge with her elbow, clearly unhappy about her cousin's rudeness in pointing out the elephant in the room. "What she means, Max," Allyson said quickly, "is that you've done a terrific job redecorating."

Though she'd tried to cover up the snark in Ashton's comment, her skepticism filtered through loud and clear: he was trying to put lipstick on a pig. Maybe so, but he'd made that pig shine! He'd gone full tilt on creating a Christmas atmosphere, too with garland, lights, poinsettia plants, and a decorated tree. He'd added a few extra touches, like the flowers in the ladies' room to encourage more women to find the place acceptable.

Smiling, Max pointed to a table near the corner specially set with a white tablecloth, spotless water glasses, and a small centerpiece made of miniature pine boughs and a scented candle. He gestured with one hand as he stared into her deep blue eyes. "Thank you. Have a seat."

The girls hung their wraps on a large coat tree and sat down at the table. Grace and Ashton sat next to each other, gesturing for Allyson to take her seat. Max tried not to stare, but when Allyson removed her shiny almond-colored ski jacket, he couldn't pull his gaze away.

Tall and slender, she looked radiant in sleek black satin slacks and a white, long-sleeved top that hugged her curves. A matching sash stretched diagonally across the front and tied at the hip, accentuating her slim waist. Her sleek blonde hair fell gracefully past her shoulders.

Maddie appeared with a metal pitcher, filling their glasses with ice and water.

"Would you girls like a cold craft beer to start your lunch?" Max asked to show them that he had more to offer than just Budweiser.

"I'll stick with water," Allyson said as she picked up her glass and took a cautious sip.

"No thank you," Grace said politely. "I'm going back to work after this. I'll take a Coke."

"Make that two," Ashton chimed in as she looked at her fitness watch, "but make mine to go. She slid from the chair and grabbed her jacket. "I just remembered that I'm supposed to be at the Chamber of Commerce meeting at City Hall at two-thirty. We've only got two weeks left to finalize the details of the Main Street celebration the downtown merchants are planning for Thanksgiving weekend." She moved to the bar to get her to-go cup. "Sorry to duck out on you like this, but I need to attend that meeting."

"I should really get going too," Grace said as she slid out of the booth and grabbed her sweater. "Mrs. Olson is tending the bar for us and waiting tables. She's a nice lady, but I'm worried about her being able to handle the place alone." She turned to Maddie standing behind the bar with the soda gun in her hand ready to pour Grace's beverage. "Never mind the Coke, Maddie. Thanks anyway!"

Allyson looked horrified. And peeved at her coworkers for suddenly abandoning her. "Ashton! Grace! What about lunch?" She glared at Grace. "You don't have to rush back to the bar. I'm sure Mrs. Olson can handle the place for an hour."

"Wait up, Ashton!" Ricky called as he rushed from the office with his jacket slung over his arm. He skidded to a stop in front of Max, his red shaggy hair falling across his forehead, nearly covering his eyes. "I forgot to tell you, Max," he said as he slipped into his jacket. "Uncle Wally made me take his place in the event committee 'cause he knew he wouldn't be here. I'll tell you all about it when I get back!"

Ashton held the door for Grace and Ricky, leaving Max and Allyson to stare at each other in shocked silence.

Chapter Five

They set me up! Allyson thought, seething at the dirty trick her cousins had just pulled on her. *Coming to this lunch was Grace's idea. How dare she drag me here and then run out on me! When I get my hands on her, I'm going to—*

Allyson grabbed her purse and began to slide out of her seat when Max placed his hand over hers, stopping her in her tracks.

"Please, don't go," he said as his gaze held hers, his deep voice echoing softly. "Lunch is ready. I promise you won't be disappointed."

She blinked several times, furiously debating what to do. She didn't want to stay but the gentle urgency in his plea gave her pause. In her heart, she knew it would be terribly rude to simply walk out on him. Besides, she and the girls had probably already given the women who patronized Trudi's salon a week's worth of juicy gossip by accepting Max's invitation in the first place. Leaving now would probably give the old biddies a good reason to sympathize with him even more—every day at lunch.

After all, she thought, justifying her reason for staying, *he went to all the trouble to set up the table with decorations and everything...*

"All right," she said slowly and dropped her purse on an empty chair. Truthfully, she was curious about how this man had completely overhauled the pool hall's reputation enough to earn rave reviews from people who wouldn't stop in on a bet before he took it over. "I'll stay."

He looked relieved as he turned to the server. "Maddie, we're ready for the first course."

Maddie silently cleared the abandoned water glasses from the table while Max slid into the chair opposite Allyson. His wide grin suggested that he wanted to smooth over their rough start. "I hope you don't mind my joining you. There is plenty of food. My cook, Rollie is so proud of this meal that he wants to make it a weekly special."

Allyson just wanted to eat and leave but she didn't want to come across as a snob, either. Besides, she was curious about Rollie's special dish. "Be my guest."

Placing his napkin on his lap, he said with a twinkle in his eye, "I think you're going to be pleasantly surprised."

"I'm counting on it," she replied, unable to keep herself from grinning back.

Maddie returned to the table with a basket of warm rolls and two freshly torn salads. She set the chilled plates on the table and left.

"This looks interesting," Allyson said and then realized she'd spoken her thoughts out loud. The plate contained romaine and arugula lettuce with dried cranberries, pecans, diced green apples, and feta cheese.

Max stared at her food with concern. "Is something wrong? Sorry, I never thought to ask you if you had any allergies."

"No, I'm fine. What I meant was," she replied, truly amazed, "I just never thought I'd get a salad like this in the town pool hall. This place has always been a burger joint."

"Rollie gets tired of flipping burgers," Max said and picked up his fork. "When I asked him if he'd like to create something special for the girls managing The Ramblin' Rose, he surprised me with a three-course menu that made me wonder why he was wasting his talent in a place like this."

"He served time in prison for drugs," Allyson replied quietly as she ate a piece of lettuce and tasted a delicious lemon vinaigrette dressing. "He got out about two years ago. Uncle Wally gave him a job when no one else in town would even be on the same side of the street with him much less employ him. He's been working here six days a week ever since."

"He cares a great deal about my uncle," Max said, grabbing a fresh roll from the basket. "What about you? I'm curious as to why you own a bar in this town. You strike me as more of a white-collar professional."

She looked up. "You're very perceptive. Yes, in the past, I owned an interior design firm in Minneapolis with a friend, and we also sold imported furniture."

"Feel free to tell me if I'm out of line for asking, but what happened? Did you sell it?"

She let out a deep breath. "It's complicated."

"Try me."

"Okay," she replied with a shrug. "It's really no secret anyway. The whole town knows what happened. You might as well, too. The business was doing great until my partner got greedy and stopped paying the bills," she said unhappily. "Before I caught on to her crooked little scheme, she'd left town with all the money. Around the same time, my boyfriend broke up with me and suddenly disappeared too." She crunched hard on a toasted pecan. "They deserve each other."

Max pried his roll apart and began to butter it. "So, if you lost all of your money, how did you acquire The Ramblin' Rose?"

Munching on her salad, Allyson sat back, not speaking until

she'd finished. "My Aunt Rose owns the building," she said at last. "She operated The Ramblin' Rose for twenty-five years. It was quite a success because she created a friendly space for people to gather. When she married Mayor Wyatt, she retired and closed the bar. The building sat empty until she gave Ashton, Grace, and me a start-up loan to revive it."

"Mayor Wyatt?" Max asked curiously. "What relation is he to Ashton and Grace?"

"He's their uncle," Allyson replied. "Their father, Bob, is the town police chief."

After a few minutes, Maddie arrived and silently removed their salad plates, giving Allyson a break from his questions. Rollie stood behind Maddie wearing a black T-shirt, jeans, and a white chef's apron. The balding man, late fifties, set two large oval plates on the table containing ceramic oven dishes.

"Chicken pot pie," he said proudly. "Made it myself this morning from scratch." He stood back. "Enjoy your lunch."

A puff of steam escaped as Allyson pierced the delicate crust with her fork. "Hmmm... It smells wonderful. Thank you, Rollie."

Once it cooled enough to eat, the creamy, rich pot pie practically melted in her mouth.

I definitely must talk to Mrs. Olson about a new menu, she thought jealously. If everything tasted this good, no wonder the gals from Trudi's were so rabid about coming here.

"So, what about you?" she asked to keep her mind from thinking about her business woes. "How are you able to take so much time off work to run this place?"

Max visibly stiffened, as though her question had touched a nerve. Whatever. She'd answered his questions. Told him things that were none of his business. Now he could answer hers.

He hesitated, his jaw clenching. "I'm currently in between jobs."

The air of tension surrounding him piqued her curiosity. There was more to that story than he'd divulged, and they both knew it. She met his uneasy expression with a pointed stare. "Care to elaborate?"

He turned his attention to his pot pie. "Not really."

"Why not?" she persisted.

He stopped pushing the crust around in his dish and glanced up. "It's complicated."

She leaned forward, chuckling. "By the look on your face, I'd say the complicating factor was a woman."

He frowned at her in disbelief. "How did you know? Are you speaking from experience or was that just a good guess?"

"It wasn't hard to put two and two together," she said with a snort. "Men are so easy to read."

One of the guys sitting at the bar suddenly choked on his beer.

Rollie appeared at their table, abruptly ending their conversation. "How's the food, folks?"

"It's wonderful, Rollie," Allyson replied with a smile. "Where did you learn to cook like this?"

"In the Navy," he said with a shrug. "I was a Culinary Specialist on an aircraft carrier."

Rollie turned his attention to Max. "So, what do you think? Do you like it?"

Max ate the last forkful and grabbed his water glass. "Congratulations, I think we've got a winner. We'll make it a weekly special."

The men shook hands on it and then Rollie disappeared into the kitchen again.

"Ready for coffee?" Maddie asked as she cleared their plates.

"Sure," Max said. "Would you like coffee, Allyson?"

"How about a pumpkin spice latte?"

He signaled to Maddie. "Make that two!"

Maddie returned in a few minutes with the lattes. Allyson had barely tasted hers before Maddie emerged from the kitchen carrying dessert. She set dishes of warm gingerbread cake garnished with a small scoop of vanilla ice cream in front of them.

Allyson picked up her fork and cut off a sliver of cake. "Wow. Rollie can bake desserts, too?"

Max laughed. "Nope. This is from Birdie's bakery."

Allyson ate her dessert in silence as her thoughts ran in a dozen different directions. All the improvements Max had instituted were good for Uncle Wally's business and bad for hers proving that she needed to step up her game and start thinking outside the box to get her customers back.

"Thank you for lunch, Max," Allyson said as she finished the last sip of her latte and placed her napkin on the table. "Give my thanks to Rollie as well. Everything was wonderful." She slid out of her chair, anxious to get back to The Ramblin' Rose and talk to Mrs. Olson.

"I'll walk you out," he murmured and pulled her jacket off the hook, holding it for her.

Once again, the gentle brush of his long fingers against her skin, this time at the nape of her neck caught her unaware, making her pulse leap as he slid the garment over her shoulders. In her haste to jam her arms into the sleeves, she accidentally planted her elbow against his rock-hard chest. "Excuse me," she blurted and looked up. The knowing look in his soft green eyes revealed that he, too, had experienced a connection. Startled by his reaction, she quickly zipped her jacket and grabbed her purse.

The front door opened, and Bernie Johnston walked in, the owner of the town's feed mill. His brows rose in surprise to see her, but he didn't say anything. Instead, he approached Max and politely introduced himself. They shook hands. Max countered by introducing himself and offering Bernie a beer on the house.

While the men spoke, Allyson slipped out the front door, glad to get away unnoticed. The chilly November air cleared her head as she stuffed her hands into her pockets and walked along Main Street to The Ramblin' Rose. West Loon Bay's small downtown had begun to take on a festive holiday scene as volunteers hung pine garlands and red velvet bows on the turn-of-the-century-style streetlamps. One block over in the city park, a small crew worked to decorate a tall Christmas tree and hang garland on the Victorian-style gazebo.

Shoving her hands deeper into her pockets, she hurried along, anxious to get back to The Ramblin' Rose and get started on a new menu to transform their business.

* * *

"She did *what*?" Allyson stomped behind the bar and kicked off her spiked heels. "No way, absolutely not!"

"It wasn't a request. Aunt Rose told the committee that she'd reserved a spot with the vendor coordinator for The Ramblin' Rose to have a booth at the festival," Ashton replied as she placed her palms on the bar. "She also said that she had already paid the fee and rented a tent. I had no idea what she had planned when she showed up at the committee meeting. I was as flabbergasted by her actions as you are."

"Who has time for that?" Allyson exclaimed, angry that Aunt Rose had volunteered the three of them to work at the festival without consulting them first. "With all the people coming downtown to see the decorations and the lighting ceremony on Thanksgiving weekend, the event could help turn us around financially. Who's going to manage the bar while we're freezing our patooties off in a booth at the festival?"

Ashton slipped onto a barstool and folded her arms, looking irritated. "Grace and I will manage the bar. *You're* managing the booth. That's Aunt Rose's plan."

Allyson leaned against the back bar and drew in a deep breath, trying to make sense of the situation. "Well, who is going to help me? Has Aunt Rose got that figured out too?"

"Actually, she does," Ashton replied with a wry smile. "She found you a partner."

"Who?"

Ashton rested her elbows on the bar and leaned forward, widening her smile. "Aunt Rose and Uncle Wally decided that you and Max will operate the booth. You're going to sell hot beverages and treats."

Allyson blinked; unsure that she'd heard correctly. "Wait…what? Me and Max Reardon? Together! Why?"

"That's what Aunt Rose wants," Ashton said. "Don't get upset with her, she's just trying to help us bring in more business. She calls Uncle Wally every day at that rehab place where he's recuperating from his knee operation. They're good friends, you know, and she's concerned about his recovery. Anyway, they thought it would be easier if both businesses shared the booth, so Uncle Wally volunteered Max, and she volunteered you."

"She should have asked me first," Allyson argued. "We can't spare anybody!"

Ashton leaned back in her chair and laughed. "Hey, look at it this way. Now you have an excuse to have lunch with Max again. I mean, you guys will have to get together to coordinate everything. This time, you can invite him here."

Allyson gazed at the floor in silence, her mind furiously spinning with a dozen reasons why sponsoring a booth was a bad idea.

"Earth to Allyson…" Ashton said in a singsong voice. "Hello!"

Allyson slowly lifted her gaze. "Look, I heard you. I realize that Aunt Rose is just trying to help us out by paying for the booth and teaming me up with Uncle Wally's nephew, but I'm not happy about this, okay? I've got enough on my to-do list already. The last thing I need is another project."

Ashton gave her a suspicious look. "Are you sure that's why you're upset? Or is it because you're attracted Max Reardon like every other woman in this town and you don't want to admit it to yourself?"

"Don't be ridiculous," Allyson snapped. Pushing herself away from the back bar, she picked up her shoes and headed for their office to research the new menu ideas that Mrs. Olson had suggested. "Let the ladies at the beauty salon swoon over him. A Duane Johnson look-alike is not my type!"

As the words left her lips Max's tall, muscular image flashed through her mind, and she almost ran into the office door. No, he wasn't her type. Sadly, a lying, cheating coward had turned out to be her type the last time around and it had made her cautious of getting involved so easily again.

Max Reardon wasn't anything like her ex-boyfriend, but regardless, her attraction to him was a waste of time. He'd made it clear yesterday that he didn't plan to stick around once his uncle was able to return to work. Besides, the guy was good-looking, smart, charming, and therefore, most likely had a girlfriend back home. A hot chick that he conveniently didn't want to talk about while they were having lunch.

Determined to put their encounter behind her, she shrugged off her negative thoughts and pushed open the office door. The sooner she got back to work, the better.

Chapter Six

November 17th

Max stared at the mess in his uncle's two-bedroom log cabin and shook his head. How Uncle Wally could live like this was beyond him. Dog hair, dust, and recyclable trash—everywhere. Talk about a fire trap. A couple of two-by-four planks were propped against the corner directly behind the oil burner and dollar store extension cords ran crisscross on the floor. As far as Max could tell, each room only had one electrical outlet.

He'd spent so much time overhauling the pool hall that he hadn't had time to deal with this place, but every night, he paid the price for putting it off with sneezing, a sniffle that wouldn't go away, and itchy eyes.

Uncle Wally never threw anything reusable away. Or put anything away. Given all the empty boxes, bags, plastic containers, and glass jars piled up in this place, bagging everything and taking it to the recycling center would take many hours, if not days. Now that he'd finished with the pool hall, however, he didn't have anything better to do, so he decided he might as well get going on it. He put on some Christmas music, uncapped a cold bottle of water, and got to work.

About an hour into his sorting and cleaning task, his cell phone rang. Thinking it might be Ricky calling with a question, he dropped the garbage bag he'd been stuffing with Styrofoam pieces and grabbed his phone. He didn't recognize the caller ID, but it didn't look like spam, so he answered the call. "Hello?"

"Well, *hello there…*"

He recognized her voice right away; that smooth, beguiling tone she always used when she wanted something from him. *Not now*, he vowed to himself. *Not ever again*.

"I told you not to call me anymore and I meant it," he warned as his jaw clenched. He'd blocked her cell phone the last time she called him and after he hung up on her this time, he'd block this number, too.

"Max, please, don't hang up. Just listen," she cajoled. "I know you're upset about what happened and I want to make it up to you, but I can't make amends if you won't talk to me. We need to meet. I promise I'll make it worth your while."

He missed his job and the great people he worked with but there was no going back to the fitness center now. "You just don't get it, do you? The damage you've done to me, to my career."

"Oh, c'mon, Max, it was only a kiss," she argued. "I'd had too much to drink on my birthday and got carried away. So what? It won't happen again."

He paced the room to keep himself from throwing something at the cabin's log wall. "You're right. It won't because I'm not coming back. So, we have nothing to talk about."

"Look, if you're worried about Leo, I can fix that," she said, becoming frustrated. "I'll tell him that you want to apologize for upsetting Susan. If you swear to him that it was just a birthday kiss and nothing more, he'll probably let it go."

The absurdity of her suggestion was so disgusting that Max almost spit a string of curse words aloud. "Look, Sybil," he said, struggling so hard to keep his temper in check that he'd begun to sweat.

He threw open the back door and tossed a full garbage bag of plastic coffee containers into the chilly back porch. The rush of frigid air into the house felt good against his face and chest but it didn't do a thing for his attitude. "You're dreaming if you think I'm going to grovel to your husband and apologize for something I didn't do. Even if I did, Leo would never trust me again and frankly, I wouldn't blame him. If I found out my wife was getting up close and personal with a trusted employee right under my nose, I wouldn't trust him again either. I'd fire him and toss him out on his—"

"Not if I talk to him, Max. As I told you before, I've got leverage over him when it comes to Skyview. I'll make sure you get the deal you deserve. I promise."

"Don't waste your time because I don't care. You've caused enough trouble for me as it is. Got that? I think we're done here."

"How dare you! After everything I've done for you, and this is the thanks I get?" she raged. "You ungrateful—"

He pulled the phone away from his ear and ended the call. Then he blocked her number and turned the phone off. And went back to tossing junk out of Uncle Wally's cabin with a vengeance.

* * *

Max stepped out the back door of the cabin to place the bag of Styrofoam and bubble wrap in the trash when he heard the commotion coming from four blocks away. Besides the laundromat, the pool hall and The Ramblin' Rose were the only two businesses open at night in downtown West Loon Bay, so it didn't take a genius to figure out where all the shouting came from.

Grabbing his jacket, he shut the door firmly and headed toward the pool hall in the cold, inky darkness. He had no way to secure the cabin's front door. Uncle Wally never locked his house and the only key that fit in the ancient, rusty door plate was somewhere on a large hoop-like ring of keys hanging in the back closet on a peg. He didn't have the patience to figure out which one turned the lock.

Large fluffy flakes whirled around him as he trudged across the street and past the city park toward the pool hall and the booming voices. The jolly shouting and raucous laughter indicated that the men weren't angry with each other, but they *were* drunk. And wherever a mob of rowdy drunks congregated, there could easily be trouble.

The guys had disappeared by the time he approached the narrow strip of parking in the back of the building. There were no tire tracks in the new snow, but a wide trail of footprints alerted him that they'd gone back inside the pool hall. He quickly slipped in through the back door, hurrying past the restrooms to the billiard hall. Dean Martin's smooth voice crooned "Baby, It's Cold Outside" over the clack-clack of billiard balls knocking against each other on the pool tables. Festive garland and blinking multi-colored lights lined the large front windows. The moment he observed the rest of the scene his bad mood went from zero to sixty in the blink of an eye.

A tall, muscular guy wearing a red buffalo plaid shirt, jeans, and a large Santa hat had his arm around a blonde server named Joy. The murderous look on her face indicated what she thought of his sloppy drunken attempt at trying to hustle up a date for himself after closing. If looks could kill, he would already be dead…

From what Max surmised, Ricky had tried to intervene, but his good deed hadn't gone unpunished. Another guy, short, husky, and bearded, wearing jeans and a bright purple Vikings sweatshirt had Ricky pinned against the wall. One purple arm braced across Ricky's neck while the other had been pulled back with the hand clenched into a fist.

"Get away from her," Max said in a steel-soft voice as he approached Joy and shoved the man's arm off her shoulders. "Don't touch her or any of my servers ever again."

Everyone stopped what they were doing and watched as the guy's eyes grew wide at the challenge. "Says who?"

Max grabbed the front of his big plaid shirt and lifted him a foot off the floor. “Says me,” he replied adding a few descriptive words to round out the conversation. “You want to make something of it?” He let go and the guy dropped clumsily to his feet looking dazed.

“Hey! You!” Max bellowed as he approached the other one and shoved him away from Ricky. “Do you want a new nose for Christmas?”

The aggressor’s bloodshot eyes attested to his drunkenness, but he was no fool. “Nah, man,” he said and backed away with his palms raised in a truce. “I don’t want no trouble with you.”

“Then back off!”

“C’mon, Len, we’re leaving this dump,” the Vikings fan said to his dazed friend. “Let’s go down to The Ramblin’ Rose and get a burger.”

The pair left by the front door with a third companion trailing behind them.

Max turned to Ricky. “You okay? That guy was pressing you pretty hard against the wall.”

“Yeah,” Ricky replied as he rubbed his windpipe. “I’m fine.”

“You’ve got to stand up to people when they get out of line,” Max said gently. “You’re in charge. Let them know that.”

“That Len Armstrong’s a bad dude,” Ricky mumbled and dropped his gaze to his feet. “That’s why he got smart with you when you told him to get away from Joy.”

“A bully always folds if you challenge him. You just need to show him that you mean business.”

“Sure,” Ricky scoffed. “A guy can do that when he’s got biceps like yours. Me, I’m a weakling. Nobody listens when I talk.”

The kid’s lack of self-esteem concerned him. “We’re going to do something about that,” Max said firmly. “I promise. But right now, I’ve got something else to do and it can't wait." He started toward the back door. "I'll see you later."

He took the back way over to The Ramblin' Rose. Once inside, he waved to Grace in the kitchen on his way to the main room. She stood at the grill in her usual jeans and T-shirt wearing a headband with reindeer antlers and a necklace of mini-Christmas lights.

Allyson stood behind the bar pouring drinks.

Her cousin, Ashton stood next to the bar talking to a tall, dark-haired man. From their casual stance, he figured the guy was her husband. As Max emerged from the kitchen, the man straightened and gave him a pointed stare, checking him out. The guy looked like he could handle himself in a pinch.

Max let out a deep breath as a flood of relief coursed through him. He'd worried about the drunks coming here and causing trouble with the girls, but Ashton's better half had the situation in hand.

"Hi, I'm Max Reardon," Max said as he approached the man with his hand extended. "I'm temporarily managing the pool hall."

"So, you're Uncle Wally's nephew," the man said with a smile and shook hands with him. "I heard about you taking over the pool hall while he was on medical leave. It's nice to finally connect the name with a face. I'm Sawyer Daniels by the way. Uncle Wally was my football coach and geography teacher in high school."

"Max," Allyson said coming up behind him. She sounded surprised. "What brings you here?"

He leaned close and whispered in her ear, "Can we talk somewhere private?"

Her eyes widened at his request. "All right. Let's go into my office."

She turned to Ashton. "Will you tend bar for a minute? Max

wants to talk to me about something."

Ashton smiled. "Sure. You guys go right ahead."

Max followed Allyson into her office and shut the door behind them.

"What's up?" she asked as she leaned against her desk with her arms folded.

"Those three guys at the bar that you just served were ejected from the pool hall a few minutes ago for getting out of line. They've had their limit of booze."

She nodded in agreement. "I can see that they're drunk, and I offered them free Cokes instead of liquor while they wait for their food. I'll see if I can get one of the other guys in the bar to drive them home."

"I just thought I should warn you about them," Max said. "They were hassling one of my servers and got rough with Ricky when he tried to intervene. When I set them straight, they decided to come down here instead."

"Thanks for your concern," she replied with a warm smile. "I'll keep an eye out for trouble and mention it to Sawyer as well. He stays until the kitchen closes and takes the girls home, so he'll be here most of the night."

Most of the night? The idea of Allyson locking up the place alone bothered him immensely. He suddenly knew where he would be at closing tonight. Waiting at the bar to escort her home safely.

* * *

Max walked into The Ramblin' Rose a few minutes before closing time and took a seat at the bar. Allyson smiled at him as she worked to break down her workstation. She wore the Santa hat that Len Armstrong had worn earlier that night.

Chris Peterson, a West Loon Bay police officer wandered

through the main area bellowing like the town crier. "Drink up, people. Time to leave. The bar's closed!"

The husky blond cop made his way to the bar. "What brings you here, Mr. Reardon," he said good-naturedly to Max. "Scoping out the competition?"

"I'm waiting for Allyson," Max said. "I'm going to escort her home tonight."

Chris' blue eyes lit up in surprise. "That's usually my job, but if she's got other plans, I'll finish clearing out the place and go back to the station. I've got paperwork to finish anyway."

"I'm surprised to see you here at this time of night," Allyson asked, looking curious as she pulled the tray from her cash drawer.

"I'm worried about those three guys who were making trouble at the pool hall," Max replied seriously. "I just want to make sure you get home safely."

She responded with a wide, beautiful smile. "Thanks for caring, but I'm not worried about them. Chris usually hangs around until I lock up and he warms up my car to make sure I get on the road without any issues."

Max scanned the room, checking to see if Len Armstrong and his cohorts were still there but they were nowhere to be found. Satisfied that they were gone, he turned back to her. "That Armstrong character showed a mean streak when I told him to leave Joy alone."

"He and his friends got a little frisky in here tonight, too," she replied as her smile faded, "but I took care of it. I know everyone in town, and they all know that I don't put up with any foolishness. If someone gets out of line and I tell them to knock it off, they understand what the consequences will be if they don't. I mean what I say."

Max leaned back in his chair, wondering how often she had to rely on Chris Peterson to back her up. "Glad to hear that. I like your hat."

She laughed and pulled it off. “Len gave it to me in place of a tip for his burger and fries. The cheapskate!”

Grabbing the cash register tray, she entered her office to lock it in the safe. When she returned, she collected all the remaining glasses on the tables while the female server on duty wiped down the tabletops and placed the chairs on top.

Once they’d finished their work and Chris and the server left for the night, Allyson pulled out her keys and locked the front door.

“Before we go,” Max said and grabbed her hand, “I want to show you a self-defense move, something that might help you if you ever find yourself in a bad situation.” When she looked at him in surprise he added, “I used to give a self-defense class for women at my old job. It was quite popular.”

She laughed and punched his arm. “I’ll bet it was!”

“Let’s go on the dance floor where we’ll have enough room to move about.”

“Why?” she replied with a nervous laugh. “Are we going to tango first?”

Sensing her apprehension, he said softly, “Don’t worry. I’m not going to put you into a hold that twists you into a pretzel. Rather, I’m going to teach you how to defend yourself to lessen the chance of someone hurting *you*.”

He walked her to the middle of the wooden floor and stopped, waiting as she kicked off her shoes. “Now turn around. I’m going to show you how to react if someone grabs you from behind.”

“Sounds ominous.” Her voice wavered with apprehension. “Do I have to do that?”

“Yes, or the exercise won’t work.”

She gingerly turned her back to him but watched him from the corner of her eye. He moved close and drew in a deep breath as he gently slid his arm around her long, delicate neck, placing the other arm behind his back. The softness of her body against the length of his heightened his senses. The fragrance of her skin filled his nostrils, making it difficult to concentrate, but he forced himself to focus. This was an important lesson. "Notice how my arm is positioned across your neck to take control of you. I could easily choke you."

She stiffened at his warning. "Yes…so what do I do?"

"All right, now grab my wrist with both of your hands and pull down on it using your full weight."

She did as he instructed, pulling his arm down.

"Be sure to turn your face to one side to protect your throat," he said urgently. "Facing forward allows your attacker to still choke you if he's strong. Now, keeping your face turned away and your hands pulling on my wrist, squat with all your weight."

She pulled downward, her soft cheek pressing against his shoulder.

"Now, lean forward as far as you can and try to get your knee behind mine."

It took her a couple of tries, but she finally succeeded in sliding her leg behind his.

"That's good," he said encouragingly. "Now grab the back of my legs and try to pull them out to knock me off balance. If that's too hard, concentrate on grabbing one with both hands. Even one can bring me down if I'm not expecting it."

She grabbed behind his knee and pulled with all her might, but he stood firm. Letting go, she straightened and turned around. "I can't do it. What am I doing wrong?"

He placed his palm on her shoulder and squeezed. "Nothing that a little practice won't fix. The more you do it, the better you'll get. The trick is, you surprise your assailant by going through the movements so fast that he doesn't have time to react."

They went through the exercise several times, each time getting faster. Max kept his arm loose across her body, taking care not to bruise her or hurt her during their practice. Even so, the longer he stood with his arm around her, the more he found it difficult to concentrate on what they were doing. So difficult, that when she suddenly grabbed his knee and pulled it out from under him, they collapsed on the floor before he realized what she'd done. Down he went with Allyson on top of him.

He lay sprawled on the dance floor, stunned as he looked up at her. With one palm resting flat on each side of his head, her face hovered above his, her eyes boring into his with shock at taking him down. His mind went blank as their gazes locked, and for a moment, neither spoke.

"I—I did it," she whispered.

He smiled awkwardly, realizing their lips were a breath apart. If he lifted his head, he could easily kiss her. But then, she could kiss him too—if she wanted to—but she didn't move. Pushing away the thought, he said, "Congratulations!"

Clearing her throat, she rolled off him and sat on the floor staring at the wooden tiles as though in a daze. He stood up and helped her to her feet.

"I think I've got it now." She stared up at him, absently brushing dust from her hands. "Thanks for showing me what to do."

"Yeah, no problem," Max said unable to look away. He needed to get out of there before he acted on impulse and pulled her into his arms. "Looks like we're done here. I'll walk you to your car."

She slipped back into her shoes and grabbed her coat from the office. They locked the building and stopped at the driver's side door of her red Mustang. "We need to get together and talk about the booth we're supposed to have at the Thanksgiving weekend event," she said sounding glum as he opened the door for her.

The words brought him back down to reality. Shoving his hands into the pockets of his hoodie, he shook his head, remembering his disappointment the day Ricky gave him the news.

Allyson tossed her purse on the seat and paused. "Are you as annoyed about this as I am?"

He let out a wry chuckle. "Let me put it this way—it wasn't on the job description when I signed up and if I had been asked first, I'd have responded with a hard no."

She laughed. "I guess there is something to the saying that misery loves company. When do you want to meet? Should we get together here? It's my turn to cook lunch."

Resting his hand on the top of the door, he hesitated then thought better of it. "I was thinking more along the order of dinner. Somewhere without a jukebox and the smell of burgers. Where we could talk without any distractions."

"I know just the place. Peterson's Resort has a wonderful restaurant, but it is a little pricey."

"Not a problem," he said with a smile. "My kind of place. Great wine and not a billiard table in sight. I'll call there tomorrow and reserve a table."

Smiling, Allyson got into her car and drove down the alley.

Max watched until her taillights disappeared wondering if he'd made a mistake by asking her to meet with him over dinner. He'd heard only good things about the food and service at Peterson's but was the setting too romantic for two people trying to ignore their attraction to each other? He didn't have a clue but neither did he have a choice. He needed to get this booth business taken care of and get back to running the pool hall until his uncle came home.

How did doing a simple favor for his mother turn into such a complicated mess?

He wished he knew.

Chapter Seven

November 18th

Allyson went over the spreadsheet one more time to make sure she hadn't missed anything, but when she finished the result was the same. Their revenue didn't cover their expenses. They didn't have enough money to pay their loan payment this month to Aunt Rose.

Heartsick, she dropped her pen on the desk and sat back with a discouraged sigh, closing her eyes as she tipped her head back. The only prospect they had for bringing in some extra cash was the booth at the festival, but that wouldn't help them this week. The festival was still almost two weeks away. Besides, it was only a temporary fix. What would they do after that if the booth didn't generate sufficient future business?

"I'm so tired," she whispered to herself. "So tired of the struggle to make ends meet. Maybe we should give up and let the place go back to Aunt Rose."

The thought of disappointing her aunt bothered her so much that she opened her eyes and sat up straight. *Not an option*, she told herself. After all Aunt Rose had done for them, she'd rather die than fail.

Grabbing her pen and notebook, she went back into the bar noting how depressing the place seemed. The quietest time of day was about an hour between the end of lunch and the beginning of happy hour. Except for employees, the bar was empty. Christmas music echoed off the walls like a holiday funeral parlor.

She found Ashton and Grace sitting at the employee table eating a family-style salad. Allyson grabbed a glass of soda water garnished with a lemon slice from the bar and walked over to the table.

"C'mon," she said to the girls as she sat down and smacked her notebook on the table. "Let's brainstorm. The newspaper ad cost a small fortune, but it didn't bring in as much business as we had hoped so we're on to Plan B." She uncapped her pen and poised her hand over the notebook. "Throw out some ideas. Go."

The girls stopped eating and stared at her like raccoons at night caught climbing out of a dumpster.

"Well?" she said becoming frustrated with their silence.

"Half-priced appetizers, special happy hour drinks, and an early-bird dinner menu," Ashton said. "We've already done all those things, and they didn't work."

Allyson gripped her pen hard, desperate to keep her temper. Getting mad wouldn't solve anything, but throttling her cousin—just once—would give her great satisfaction. Instead, she turned to Grace. "What about you?"

Grace finished eating her salad and set down her fork. "As if anybody really listens to me!"

"Hey," Allyson argued, "I'm listening now. What ideas do you have?"

Grace's mouth curved downward in a pout. "The same ideas that you and Ashton trashed last time we had this discussion. My beer batter onion rings are popular, so I want to sell a jumbo basket and two beers for a special price on the regular menu. I also want to make a taco plate and a giant hot beef sandwich with real mashed potatoes and gravy. Oh, and a walleye sandwich coated with my beer batter. Make it a platter with coleslaw and seasoned steak fries."

Allyson stared at her, wondering why she hadn't gone along with those ideas before. "Really? Okay, it's a deal."

Grace pulled her napkin off her lap and dropped it on her empty plate. "And I want to bring back the soup and salad bar."

"That's a lot of prep work and clean up," Ashton argued. "The staff time it takes to prepare it is why we stopped doing it in the first place."

"And that's when a lot of women quit coming in here for lunch," Grace snapped. "All we do around here is cater to men!"

Allyson held up her palms to take down the temperature of the discussion. Grace had scored an interesting point. Women had stopped coming into the bar to eat when Max took over managing the pool hall and that was about the time they decided to quit offering the salad bar. The ratio of women to men needed to change. "Okay, let's do it."

Allyson and Grace stood up to leave.

"Wait a minute," Ashton said impatiently. "I think we should dress nicer too. Just until the holidays are over. Ditch the jeans and T-shirts." She stood and grabbed her empty plate. "What about you, Allyson? What ideas do you have?"

Allyson pushed in her chair. "I'm going to put together a special holiday cocktail list. Fun drinks to entice female customers to stop in with their friends after work." She sighed, feeling better already. They had a long way to go to get things back on track, but at least they had some promising ideas. This was their last chance to save The Ramblin' Rose.

* * *

Business picked up over happy hour, but the dinner crowd was sparse. Sawyer dropped in later that night to take Ashton and Grace home. He sat at the bar wearing black jeans and a red, long-sleeved shirt under his favorite black leather bomber jacket. His glossy kohl hair, thick and wavy, brushed the collar of his coat. The permanent shadow darkening his jaw amplified his edgy, bad-boy look.

But the first thing she noticed about him was the grim expression on his face.

"What's with the grumpy face?" Allyson asked as she poured him a frosty mug of beer. She set it in front of him and walked around the bar, slipping onto the barstool next to him. "Is something wrong?"

"We need to talk," he said quietly and sipped his beer, "about the future of The Ramblin' Rose."

Grace suddenly appeared carrying an oval plate containing three crispy mini-tacos. "Hey, you're just in time to try my newest appetizer. Taste it and let me know what you think!"

Sawyer picked up one of the mini-tacos and stuffed half of it in his mouth. With his mouth full, he merely nodded with a smile.

"Great! Enjoy!"

Allyson waited until Grace went back into the kitchen before picking up the conversation again. "What were you saying about The Ramblin' Rose?"

Sawyer washed down the rest of his taco with his frosted beer. "I know how hard you and the girls have worked to make this place a success. I've always been supportive of you since day one and I've tried to help in any way I can, but you've been in a slump for some time now and things don't seem to be getting better. I guess what I mean is, the situation is getting to the point where you've got to either get a good breakthrough strategy or call it quits."

His lecture stunned her. Of all the people in her life, Sawyer Daniels, her lifelong friend, was the one person she thought would always support her no matter what. Her parents did, and Aunt Rose did.

What was with his sudden change of heart?

“Wow.” Resting her elbows on the bar, she stared into his coffee-colored eyes. “What brought this on?”

Sawyer let out a deep sigh. “I see how much energy it takes out of Ashton working long hours day in and day out and I wonder if the stress is worth it.”

“Every business has ups and downs,” she countered. “We’re working on it. You have to be patient. It takes time.”

“That’s what concerns me the most,” Sawyer said and took another swig of his beer. “You know that Ashton and I are looking at design plans for a new house next summer and one of these days we’re going to want to have a kid.” He turned to her. “How can Ashton and I build a life together if she’s spending all of her time here trying to revive this dead horse?”

Tears clawed at the back of Allyson’s eyes, but she held them back. “We’re doing the best we can, Sawyer.”

“I know you are, but I’m worried about Ashton. She can’t continue to work like this much longer.” He slipped his arm around her shoulders and gave her a gentle squeeze. “I love you, kid. You’ve always been like a sister to me, and I don’t mean to discourage you, but the health and happiness of my wife is my main priority now. Ashton and I have talked it over and we—”

“Wait—” Allyson blurted in surprise, interrupting him. “Why are *you* telling me this? Why didn’t she come to me and tell me herself?”

“You and she are too much alike and you’ll just butt heads,” Sawyer replied. “We need you to understand that it isn’t personal. We have to start putting money away for our future or the house and the kid will never happen. So, we’ve come to a decision. You and the girls have until the end of the year to turn this place around. If not, Ashton is done here. She’s going to partner with me at my construction company.”

"But…she doesn't know anything about the construction business!"

Sawyer drained the last of his beer and shoved the mug aside. "She didn't know anything about the bar business when you guys opened this place, either, but she learned. She can do the same thing again in construction. I can offer her a steady job with better pay, nine to five, and no weekends. Best of all, we'll have more time to spend together."

Ashton wanted to leave The Ramblin' Rose? A surge of panic gripped Allyson's heart. If Ashton left, Grace would probably follow, leaving her to struggle with this place alone.

She slid from the bar stool in a daze, weighed down by the ugly truth. Without her cousins, The Ramblin' Rose would fail for sure. She couldn't let that happen.

She had to work harder than ever to save it.

Chapter Eight

Friday, November 22nd

Max sat in his office working on the payroll when loud voices from the main room jarred his thoughts. Curious, he leaned back in his chair and cracked open the door to listen to the commotion.

"Where's my ketchup? Hey, moron, I told you to get me a new bottle five minutes ago!"

He didn't recognize the voice but knew the guy had to be in Len Armstrong's gang of bullies. They'd come in for lunch and all of them were sitting at the bar when Max went into his office to get some paperwork done. Their loud voices were obnoxious at best when they were joking around, but the ugliness he'd just heard coming from someone spelled trouble.

What's going on now? If I have to go out there and settle another fight with those guys, I'm going to knock some heads together...

He'd been out of sorts ever since his self-defense lesson with Allyson landed him on the floor with her soft, curvy body sprawled on top of him. He'd come so close to putting his arms around her and kissing her. So close! Resisting the temptation to get involved with her had been the right thing to do. The practical side of his brain knew that, but the emotional side didn't care, and thoughts of *what if* had been bombarding him ever since, making him grumpy.

The *crack* of a glass smashing on the bar was the last straw. Max leaped out of his chair and stormed out of his office. In the dining room, he found Ricky working furiously to mop up spilled beer. The liquid had covered the bar and dripped onto a bar stool. Off to one side, one of the Armstrong gang stood wringing a draft Budweiser out of his shirt.

Max approached the man. "What happened?"

The man looked up, a snarl darkening his bushy eyebrows and scruffy beard. "What, are you blind?" He pointed at Ricky. "This incompetent piece of—"

He didn't like it when people picked on Ricky, but he wouldn't tolerate any disrespect aimed at him from these jokers. One deadly look from Max abruptly silenced the guy. Instead, the man redirected his glare at Ricky, sending him a silent message of promised retribution.

Max turned to one of the female servers. "Maddie, would you please finish cleaning up this mess for me? Thanks. Ricky—in my office. *Now.*"

He went back to his office with Ricky trailing close behind, head down, imaginary tail between his legs.

"When you're done here, get me some ketchup and be quick about it," he heard the man tell Maddie. "My lunch is getting cold."

"Who died and made you king? Get it yourself," she snapped loud enough to wake the dead. "There's one at the end of the bar."

The pool hall went uncharacteristically silent.

Max shut the door to his office.

Ricky all but cowered in the corner. "I'm sorry, Boss, I didn't mean to knock that glass over—"

"Never mind that now," Max said cutting him off. "It's not important. Ricky, you've got to stand up for yourself. Did you hear how Maddie just put that jerk in his place? That's the reason why I'm training her to become an assistant manager along with you. She doesn't take any guff from the guys who try to give her trouble and neither should you."

"Yeah, but Boss, she's a woman! They wouldn't dare do anything to her."

"She only weighs a hundred pounds soaking wet, but no one tries to take advantage of her, and you want to know why?" Max leaned against his desk, softening his stance. "She commands respect from her peers, and you should, too."

Ricky frowned and stared at his feet. "I know… I've been working out every day with the weights like you showed me."

"Hey," Max said gently, placing his large palm on Ricky's shoulder. "That's great. Just keep it up. You'll get there."

One of the first things he'd organized after the storeroom had been cleaned out was to set up a small, temporary gym so he could work out every morning. He'd given Ricky permission to use the equipment with the hope that it would strengthen not only his body but his self-esteem as well.

Ricky nodded.

"In the meantime, I don't want you to take any more insults from *anyone*, understand? Command respect."

"But Boss…"

"Don't worry. I'll back you up." He clapped Ricky on the shoulder. "C'mon. Let's find out if Rollie has any chicken pot pie left. I'm starving. How about you?"

Max opened the door and stood aside for Ricky to go first, deliberately ignoring the stack of paperwork sitting on his desk. It could wait. He'd temporarily dealt with Ricky's problem, but he needed a break to keep his mind off his disastrous self-defense lesson with Allyson and their upcoming dinner meeting as well. Common sense dictated that the best solution for him was to stay in the pool hall and mind his own business until Uncle Wally came home, but his uncle had spent money on the booth and was counting on him.

So, he was stuck.

* * *

Saturday, November 23rd

Max pulled into the parking lot of Peterson's Resort and scanned the area for a shiny red Mustang. He didn't see it anywhere. Allyson had insisted on driving herself to dinner. After a few tense moments of wondering whether she'd bailed on him, he saw it parked in the valet lot.

His watch displayed seven o'clock on the dot. Wondering how long she'd been there, he parked his car and hustled into the wide lobby decorated with twinkling lights, fragrant pine boughs, and a seven-foot Christmas tree. He found her sitting in an overstuffed chair in front of a fire roaring in a huge split boulder fireplace near the resort registration desk. She didn't see him at first, but his chest tightened as he took in every detail of her from the sparkly black dress that hugged her curves to the shimmering waves in her soft blonde hair.

"Hello," he said quietly as he approached her.

She looked up at the sound of his voice. "Hello."

Something had changed between them and though he didn't know why, it made him uncomfortable. The uncertain look in her eyes alerted him that she sensed it as well.

"Shall we go?" Deftly ignoring the tension enveloping them, he offered his hand to help her stand. The moment their palms locked together his pulse hammered erratically. He assisted her and then let go before his hand began to perspire, revealing his nervousness.

He walked her to The Cove restaurant, keeping his hands in his pockets until they were seated at a table in the corner. Sitting across from him, her dress and hair sparkled under the holiday lights, highlighting her creamy skin and deep blue eyes more than ever.

Their server arrived at the table bearing a bottle of white wine. “May I interest you in a bottle of Riesling this evening?”

“Sure,” Max said quickly then regretted his impulsivity. “Is that all right with you Allyson, or would you like something different?”

She shrugged and smiled at the server. “Sounds fine to me. I love a good Reisling.”

Once the server finished pouring the wine, Max held up his glass, grateful to have something right away to take the edge off his nerves. “Shall we toast to a successful event?”

Allyson held up her glass to match his. “Successful and swift! I can’t wait to get it over with.”

He couldn’t help but laugh at her honesty. “Yeah, me too.”

The hum of conversation across the dining room and the tinkling of silverware blending with soft strains of classical Christmas music masked the awkward silence that descended over them as they drank their wine.

“I’m curious about something,” Allyson said suddenly. She stared at her wine glass as though she had something pressing on her mind. “When we had lunch at the pool hall, I told you why I came back to West Loon Bay and revived The Ramblin’ Rose with my cousins. When I asked you why you left your job, I guessed it was because of a woman, but when I pressed you on it, you weaseled out of talking about it with a lame excuse.” She swirled the wine left in her glass. “‘It’s complicated,’ you said. At the time, I understood that you didn’t want everyone in the pool hall getting all the juicy details of your love life. Now that we’re away from there, would you care to explain?”

“All right,” Max said and drained the rest of his wine. “I’m—I *was* the gym manager in a luxury fitness center and a personal trainer for special clients. The woman was my boss' wife. I know what you're thinking and no, I wasn't sleeping with her. I left the job because I *didn't* want to have an affair with her. She made it clear that if I wanted a promotion, it would be on her terms. So, I walked."

"Why didn't you just say no?"

Max shook his head emphatically. "Not to *that* woman. Sybil is used to getting everything she wants, and she had her sights set on me. I'm not going to sleep with *anybody* just to get ahead. Even if I wanted to," he said grimly, "her jealous husband is not a man to betray. He employs bodyguards who are more ripped than me and he would have no qualms about taking me down if he found out that I'd messed around with his wife."

"Wow. And I thought I had problems," she mused with a sympathetic smile as the server dropped off their menus.

Max picked up the leatherbound folder and opened it. "Not a problem anymore. She's long gone."

They had finished dinner and were drinking coffee when they began their discussion on participating in the festival.

"So," Allyson announced as she pulled a small notebook and a pen from her purse. "Let's start with what we're going to serve. That will dictate what equipment we need."

"All right," Max said, thinking this would be the easy part.

Allyson reached into her purse again. "I've done some research, and I've got a great list of holiday drinks we can sell." She unfolded the list and began to skim over it. "Pumpkin Spice White Russian, Bourbon and cider garnished with a slice of apple, White Christmas Margarita…" She looked up. "What's wrong?"

"This is a family event for one thing," he said dryly. "If people want alcohol, they can go to the pool hall or the bar. That sounds like a great list for you to promote in The Ramblin' Rose, but not in our booth.

For one thing, we'd probably have to pay for a special permit to serve alcohol and that would cut into our profit. Besides, it's too much of a hassle to check IDs."

She looked unhappy but let it go. "Okay, what do you suggest?"

"Beverages we can pour easily from an urn like hot cider and coffee, and boiling water for hot chocolate. Cans of soda, bottles of water. Fast and family friendly. Lots of profit."

"Okay," she said and wrote it down on her list. "You mentioned coffee. Specialty coffee would be a big hit."

Max shook his head. "Too labor intensive. We want to make as much money as we can in the few hours we have and that's not the way to do it."

She exhaled a big sigh to let him know what she thought of him overriding her ideas. "Moving along to appetizers," she said. "We could sell hot cheese nachos."

"According to Ricky, someone is already selling pizza, hot dogs, and nachos," Max argued. "I say we sell premade treats like Rice Krispie bars, cookies, and fudge. Stuff we don't have to make ourselves."

"Well, I'm putting my foot down on this one," Allyson snapped. "We're selling gift certificates!"

"Sure," Max countered with a grin, "as long as the purchaser gets a coupon for two free drinks with the certificate as an incentive to buy it."

She dropped her notebook on the table and tossed her pen in his direction. "You're impossible!"

The pen bounced off his chest and landed on his lap. Laughing, he picked it up and handed it back to her. "C'mon, Allyson, I'm just trying to keep this project as painless as possible. The less setup and takedown we have to do, the better."

He paid the check and as they walked into the lobby, they came upon a young woman wearing an elf costume with brightly rouged cheeks handing out candy canes. She gave them each one and then pointed upward to a sprig of mistletoe. “Merry Christmas!”

Before Max realized that Allyson might not like what he was doing, he’d placed his hand upon the nape of her neck, angled his head, and drew her toward him. As their mouths joined, he realized he’d wanted to do this since the first time they met. Her lips were soft and moist, parting slightly as he kissed her with a tenderness that revealed more about his attraction to her than he wanted to admit. He didn’t know when he’d fallen for her—perhaps it had been gradual—but knowing what he knew now, he’d never be the same again.

Chapter Nine

Allyson stood frozen as Max's lips collided with hers. She knew it was coming when he placed his hand on the back of her neck, but when it happened, it still took her by surprise. She closed her eyes, thinking he'd give her a peck on the lips and get it over with, but he took his time. Placing his mouth firmly upon hers, he leaned into her, kissing her with the skill of a man who knew how to convey his innermost feelings, and right now he revealed that he was irresistibly drawn to her.

Too soon, he slowly pulled back, leaving her shaken and confused.

Another elf stepped forward with a camera, breaking the spell. "Here's the image," she said and held out the camera for them to see the digital photo.

The picture produced a thousand words, all pointing to one conclusion—the couple kissing looked like they were falling in love.

"You two look so sweet together," she said to Allyson. "Are you newlyweds?"

She and Max began to sputter protests at the same time.

"If you'd like to have the photo emailed to you," the elf happily chirped, "I'll need twenty-five dollars and your email address."

"N-no thanks," Allyson mumbled, stumbling away from the bubbly, ruddy-cheeked elves as fast as she could. She headed toward the coat check with her ticket in her hand, desperate to get her jacket and get away from this place.

Max quickly caught up to her. He shoved a couple of bills into the tip jar and helped Allyson into her coat. He didn't speak as he walked her to the valet stand to get her car, causing her to wonder if he regretted his impulsiveness as much as she did. They waited inside the entrance until a young man pulled up in her red Mustang and jumped out. Max opened the heavy glass door shielding them from the cold winter night and walked her to the car.

He stopped at the open car door, placing his hand along the top. "Allyson, I—"

She looked up, waiting for his apology. Or something else…

"Ah…drive carefully. There are a lot of deer roaming about this time of night."

She nodded. "Thanks, I will."

They stared into each other's eyes, their silence speaking volumes. The desire in his eyes left no doubt in her mind that he wanted to kiss her again, but at the same time, she sensed his resistance. Ironically, an identical push/pull of emotional turmoil battled inside of her too. She wanted nothing more than to repeat what had happened under the mistletoe, but she knew it was foolish to get involved with a man who wasn't going to be around much longer.

"Um…lady," the young valet said, "there's another car behind you waiting to pull up."

A reality check by an eighteen-year-old.

"Sure," Allyson said and dug into her pocket for a couple of loose bills. She handed the tip to the teen and slid into the driver's seat. Max said he'd call her if he had any last-minute issues with the booth and shut the door for her. Stepping away, he stayed in her rear-view mirror, looking strangely troubled as she drove off.

On the drive home, she took deep breaths and began to relax, relieved that he hadn't acted on his impulses.

"Getting involved with him is the last thing I need," she grumbled to herself. She had enough problems without adding a short-term fling to the mix.

Even so, she couldn't deny a surge of disappointment lurking in the corners of her heart.

* * *

Sunday, November 24th

A few minutes before the bar opened, Allyson twisted her long blonde hair into a messy bun and tied it with a red satin ribbon to match her white knit top and red stretch jeans. Jingle bell earrings tinkled from her ears, creating music every time she turned her head. She slipped her feet into flat, Mary Jane shoes and pulled on a white chef's apron to complete her holiday look.

The Vikings were playing the Packers today, a good sign that the bar would be filled with exuberant fans. With their new holiday specials, hopefully, the kitchen would be busy too. Last March, they'd splurged on a huge new television in time for the Stanley Cup playoffs and paid someone to mount it on the back wall of the bar. On big game days like today, it drew so many fans that it had already paid for itself.

Grace walked out of the kitchen and stood at the bar, her eyes filled with confusion and uncertainty. "I need your help. The dishwasher isn't working…"

Allyson raced out from behind the bar. "What? What's wrong with it?"

"I don't know," Grace mumbled. "When I turn it on, the machine hums, but it doesn't wash."

"No," Ashton cried as she dropped her bar towel on a table and hurried into the kitchen. "Not today, of all days!"

Ashton tried to start the huge machine, but it acted just as Grace described. Smacking her hands on top of her head, she spun around. "Now what are we going to do? We can't get someone to fix it today unless we pay them extra for coming out on a Sunday. That is if anyone is available at the last minute!"

"Even if we could get a repairman," Grace argued, "we can't afford to keep fixing this dinosaur. It's worn out!"

Ashton stared at a stack of dirty dishes from Grace's prep work. "So, what should we do?"

"The obvious," Allyson said as she grabbed a full bus pan. "We wash them by hand."

Ashton's face flushed scarlet. "All day?" She glanced at a couple of dirty pots and pans that Grace had piled on the counter. "Are you kidding me?"

Grace walked over to the divided, stainless-steel sink and turned on the hot water. "No, she's not. I'll clean up my mess and when Darren gets here, I'll help him keep up whenever I can, but you guys need to do your share of dishwashing, too."

In an uncharacteristic fit of temper, Ashton pulled off her apron and tossed it in the dirty towel bin. "That's it. I'm done."

"Where are you going," Allyson cried as Ashton stormed out of the kitchen. In shock, she and Grace followed Ashton into the bar. "We've got a mess to clean up!"

"Not me. I quit!"

To Allyson's horror, Ashton went into the office and grabbed her coat. "I'm going to get a real job working for my husband with breaks and a good paycheck!" she snapped as she stomped toward the front door.

"She'll be back," Grace said dryly and went back to the sink to scrub pots and pans.

As Allyson watched Ashton leave, her heart sank, and she wondered how they would manage without her.

Chapter Ten

November 28th – Thanksgiving Weekend

Max stood inside his rectangular tent at the festival on Main Street and checked his equipment to make sure the extra-large circuit breaker power strip he bought at Strom's hardware store in town for this occasion had been plugged into the generator. He'd also purchased several for his uncle's cabin along with heavy extension cords to improve the situation there. The dollar store cords, and cheap electrical strips had gone straight into the trash.

His employees had moved tables, two chairs, and all the equipment they needed into the tent for him, including a large, thick rug to cover the asphalt and keep their feet from freezing. They'd stocked the tent with all the ingredients for hot drinks and brought in large boxes of treats. An electric heater in the corner kept them warm. Several shop lights hung from the upper framework filling the tent with bright light. Under one of the tables, Sandy lay curled up in his soft dog bed. The front of the tent had a wide opening where they would serve their customers.

In the city park, located in the center of town, a huge crowd gathered to listen to Mayor Wyatt kick off the holiday festivities in the gazebo with his seasonal address and then cheer has he flipped the switch to light up the town's two-story Christmas tree. As part of the official ceremony, a large choir from one of the local churches sang Christmas carols. Their angelic voices permeated the air with "O Holy Night."

Allyson burst into the tent shortly after the opening address began wearing jeans, a white shirt, and a gold sweater. He hadn't spoken to her since the night they had dinner. Since then, Ricky had served as their go-between, taking on the task of coordinating every detail and scheduling staff to handle the setup and takedown.

"Sorry, I'm late," she said breathlessly. "We're short-handed at the bar."

Max pulled a stack of Styrofoam cups from a box of supplies under the tables and set them next to the coffee urn. Several days earlier, Ricky had heard one of the ladies from the beauty salon gossiping during lunch that Allyson's cousin had become upset about something and walked out. "So, Ashton hasn't returned to The Ramblin' Rose yet?"

Allyson shook her head. "No, she's working for Sawyer now. She's out of the business altogether."

The sadness in her eyes tugged at his heartstrings. It bothered him to see her so unhappy and he wished he could do something to convince Ashton to return but it wasn't his place to interfere.

Once the tree-lighting ceremony ended and the crowd descended upon them, they were too busy selling beverages and treats to happy festivalgoers to engage in conversation. It was just as well. After the disastrous way their dinner date ended, Max realized he needed to keep his distance. After tonight, he had no plans to interact with Allyson ever again. The notion that he'd never see her again bothered him immensely, but he pushed the thought away. He planned to go back to Minneapolis as soon as his uncle returned home and get prepared to look for a new job. It made no sense to start something with her that he couldn't finish.

Toward the end of the evening, Allyson's Aunt Rose and her husband, Mayor Hugh Wyatt, stopped into the tent for a few minutes to say hello. As Rose chatted with Allyson, she didn't mention Uncle Wally, but Max had a notion that his uncle would be getting a full report from her tomorrow about the success of the booth.

The event lasted until nine o'clock, but by eight-thirty, when Rose and Hugh stopped by, the crowd had begun to thin considerably. Families with young children had disappeared. Down the street, the huge chair where Santa and his helpers had entertained people sat empty. Only older couples and groups of teens remained.

At around nine o'clock, Mayor Wyatt appeared holding a magnum of sparkling wine and a carrying case filled with stemmed glasses. He held up the bottle and began pouring the wine into two glasses. "Merry Christmas! Thank you both for doing your part in making this event the first of many to come!"

Before they had the chance to thank him, he'd set the glasses on the serving counter and moved on to the next booth.

Max held up his glass in a toast. "Merry Christmas. We survived."

Allyson laughed as she touched the rim of her glass to his and then sipped the bubbly liquid. "Hmmm…this is *very* good sparkling wine. Just what I needed to wind down." She leaned out of the serving window, looking down the street. "I wonder where the mayor went. I'd like to get some more." By that time, however, he had disappeared.

Max laughed. "Oh, well. Bottoms up."

He tipped his head back, savoring the semi-sweet liquid as it slid down his throat and warmed his chest. Suddenly, he froze. "What's that?"

Allyson finished her wine and looked up, her mouth gaping. "Who did that?" She glared at him. "Did you? Is this some kind of joke?"

"No," Max exclaimed in self-defense. "I didn't put it there, I swear. It must have been one of my staff."

A small sprig of mistletoe fastened with a thin red ribbon to the framework hung directly above their heads. Seeing it brought back memories of the night they'd kissed at the restaurant and the earthquake that had erupted in his heart, destroying his peace forever.

Staring into her eyes, he set his glass on the counter, barely aware that she had set hers down too. Without hesitation, his arms slid around her waist as her hands locked behind his neck. Ever since she walked into the tent, he'd struggled to push away thoughts of kissing her again. Now that he had a second chance to show her what she meant to him, he had no intention of wasting one moment in indecision. Pulling her close, he crushed his lips upon hers, kissing her with a passion he'd never experienced before.

"Oh, Max," she whispered, pulling away. "We can't—"

"Yes, we can," he said and kissed her again. "Ever since I kissed you at the resort, I've barely been able to function, much less accomplish anything. Why do you think Ricky took over the project? I've been a basket case trying to act normal. I can't do it anymore."

"But, Max," she said breathlessly, "if you're moving back to Minneapolis when your uncle returns, where does that leave us?"

"We'll make it work," he said crushing her to his chest. "I don't know how yet, but we'll figure it out."

They came together again, sealing their newly found happiness with a deep, fiery kiss.

"Uh…Boss?"

They jerked apart to find Ricky standing outside the tent, peering through the serving window, red-faced. "Sorry to interrupt, but the festival is over and all of the booths are closing down. You want me to round up the crew and start cleaning up?"

Max cleared his throat. "Ah…right…go ahead," he mumbled while straightening his shirt.

Ricky left to gather up his coworkers, leaving Max and Allyson alone again. They burst out laughing.

"Well," Allyson said as she leaned against his chest and toyed with a button on his light blue shirt. "I guess that's that. By tomorrow it'll be all over town that Ricky caught us locking lips. I wonder what the ladies at Trudi's salon will have to say about it."

"Probably quite a bit," Max said with a belly laugh. "It saves us the trouble of telling everyone, right?"

She gave him a tentative smile. "As long as you're serious…"

"You bet I am," Max said, framing her face with his hands. "I've never been more intentional about anything in my life."

* * *

Later that evening, after Max left Ricky and his crew to finish cleaning out the tent so the rental company could dismantle it in the morning, he wearily trudged home with Sandy in tow. It had been a long day, and he was beat, but not too tired to shower and throw on clean clothes. He planned to drop in on Allyson at The Ramblin' Rose at closing time and take her to an all-night café in Summerville. Now that they were together, they had a lot to talk about and he wanted to get her opinion of an idea he had about starting a new business—a fitness center.

It had begun to snow. A steady flow of flakes whispered in the night as they fell all around him, covering the street and dusting everything with a coat of pristine white. The houses he passed by were dark. All was quiet except for the sound of his footfalls. West Loon Bay had retired for the night.

Sandy stopped occasionally to sniff the tire of a car or lift his leg against a tree. Max patiently indulged the old boy.

He rounded the corner. Up ahead, Uncle Wally's log cabin loomed in between two houses; one old, one new. A sliver of light shone between the curtains in the cabin's bedroom window.

That's strange, he thought. *I don't remember leaving the light on.* Oh, well. He'd left the house early that morning to get ready for the festival and probably forgot to turn it off.

He opened the front door and stood aside to let the dog in. Sandy walked stiff legged into the living room and stopped, sniffing the air.

His odd behavior caused Max to pause. "What's the matter, boy?"

A ridge of golden hair stood up on Sandy's back. "Woof! Woof!"

Max's senses sharpened. Someone was in the house. In the bedroom. He looked around for something to use as a weapon and he wished he'd left the boards standing in the corner behind the oil burner. They would have either caught fire and burned the house down by now or provided him with a good weapon to take out this intruder.

Shuffling sounds coming from the bedroom alerted him that it was too late to look for a weapon. His fists clenched. He needed to make do with what he had.

Suddenly a shadow appeared in the doorway and Sybil King moved into view wearing nothing but his white button-down shirt with the sleeves rolled back to her elbows. All the buttons were undone except the middle one. She'd tied her dark curly hair atop her head with a ribbon. One hand clutched an open bottle of wine. The other held her wineglass.

She smiled beguilingly. "Hello, Max."

His jaw dropped. *What the—* He blinked in disbelief. *No...*

Laying his ears back, Sandy began to growl.

Too shocked to speak, Max stared at her face, refusing to let his gaze drop lower. His anger flared as an emotional trap door opened, and his patience dropped through. "What are you doing here?" he demanded once he found his voice.

She set down the bottle and glass on the dresser and with her arms folded, she leaned against the doorframe in a sexy pose. "What do you think?"

"I don't know what to think when it comes to you, Sybil. You defy logic."

"Well," she said as she sauntered toward him. "If I have to tell you what I want, you're not the man I thought you were."

"You're right. I'm not. So, get dressed. And leave."

"Baby, it's cold outside," she crooned as she approached him. She coyly slid her arms around his neck. Then she ran her tongue over her full red lips. "I'm not going anywhere."

He grabbed her by the wrists and jerked her arms away. "How did you find me?" he demanded. Without waiting for an answer, he walked into the bedroom to round up her clothes.

"Your mother is a very nice lady, but not too bright," Sybil replied with a derisive chuckle. "She volunteered the information without questioning my reason for wanting it."

"I don't appreciate you using her to get back at me," he snapped as he walked around the bed, picking female garments off the floor. Once he'd collected them all, he crushed them into a ball and threw it at her. "I said, get dressed. *Now.* You're leaving."

Letting the clothes fall back to the floor, she flopped on the bed with an exaggerated sigh. "Can't. Too much wine." She laughed loudly at her predicament. "I need a good nap before I drive all the way back to Minneapolis." She patted the space next to her. "I'll sleep better if you join me."

Gripping his hands on his hips, he stared at her, disgusted by her gall. "Leo wouldn't be happy if he knew you were here."

She laughed again. "Do you have any idea what he'd do to *you* if he found out? I don't think you want him to know. He's already angry that you made a pass at me on my birthday."

"Is that what you told him?" He'd had enough. It was time to call her bluff. He picked up the phone. "Let's find out."

Sybil went still and watched him, obviously waiting to see if he meant to go through with the call. Her eyes widened in panic when he dialed the number. She bolted upright and tried to grab the phone away from him. "Max, don't! We need to talk first. Please!"

Max stubbornly turned his back on her.

Leo answered on the first ring. "You're just the person I want to talk to, Reardon," he said in his raspy voice. "I'm disappointed in you for walking out on your job at the club without talking to me first."

"I didn't feel like apologizing for something I didn't do or groveling to get my job back. It isn't worth sacrificing my self-respect," Max stated boldly. "I'm simply calling to let you know that on her way to destroy someone else's life, Sybil got lost and ended up on my doorstep." He paused, waiting for Leo's reaction. Nothing but crickets. "She's drunk," he continued, "so you need to come and get her."

"Give me the address." Leo sounded tired. Not physically tired, but the kind of exhaustion a person developed under constant stress.

Max told Leo where he could pick up his wife in detailed instructions.

"She's in West Loon Bay? What is she doing there?" Leo let out a string of cuss words. "She must have found out that I… Never mind. I'm already on my way. I'll be there in about a half hour."

Max pulled the phone from his ear and stared at it in disbelief. He's only thirty minutes away? That meant he'd also planned a trip to West Loon Bay. Were these two in cahoots somehow? Why?

"Fine. See you there," Max barked and hung up. He slammed the phone on the dresser and turned to Sybil. "I'll be in the kitchen making a sandwich. Get dressed! We're going to meet Leo at the pool hall in a half hour and get this over with."

He wanted to be in a public place when he turned Leo's wife over to him. A place with witnesses and a few of the local guys to back him up if need be. He didn't know what was going on, but something in Leo's response didn't ring true. Leo sounded disturbed by Sybil's actions when he should have been angry. Why? Was Leo saving his wrath for when they were face to face? Max had no idea, but just the same, he had a bad feeling about this.

He'd spent so much time encouraging Ricky to be strong and face his antagonists.

Now it was Max's turn.

Chapter Eleven

Allyson sat alone in her office dividing the cash they'd taken in from the festival tonight. Max had been right about keeping their products simple. It allowed them to work fast, serving a lot of people in the short time they had. Their booth had been popular, and they'd nearly sold out of everything by the time the festival ended.

Likewise, according to Grace, the bar had seen a nice bump in revenue too. More than enough to cover the payroll and make their payment this month to Aunt Rose.

But not enough left over for a down payment on a new dishwashing unit.

She sighed in discouragement. Running this place was such a struggle. One month their revenue shot up, and the next month it plummeted. Would she ever figure out how to turn the place around like Max did with the pool hall?

She glanced at her fitness watch. It was only ten o'clock. Max would probably be at the pool hall tending bar while his employees cleaned and put away all the equipment from the booth. She stared at the piles of bills on her desk and sighed, too tired to make out a deposit for the bank. It had been a long and extra busy day. This could wait until tomorrow morning when the bar was quiet, and her mind had become refreshed by a good night's sleep. She gathered everything up and locked it in the safe.

Grace had hired extra staff to handle the bar tonight and her presence wasn't needed for once. It felt good to have a few hours to herself, especially given how tired she was. She suddenly had an idea.

Why don't I go down to the pool hall and visit Max? It would be nice to be on the other side of the bar for a change.

Pulling off her old jeans, she changed into a pair of red skinny jeans, red pumps and a shimmering pearl knit top with a silver belt. Like Aunt Rose did when she operated the bar, Allyson and the girls kept a small wardrobe in the office to change into a new outfit whenever they had a special event going on or needed to attend a business meeting.

She pulled the envelope with Max's half of the festival proceeds out of the safe and stuffed it into her purse.

Earlier, people coming into the bar had been covered in light, flaky snow. She didn't want to walk into the pool hall looking like a snowman, so she wound a light scarf around her head. Grabbing her purse, she slipped on her coat, turned off the light, and locked the door.

"I'm going down to the pool hall to see Max," she told Grace on her way out. "I want to find out who hung that mistletoe in the ceiling of the tent!"

Word had already gotten back to Grace about kissing Max in the booth. Everyone in the bar knew about it! Grace merely laughed and shook her head. "Good luck!"

Most of the patrons in the bar stared at Allyson as she walked through the main room and left by the front door. Let them gawk. It wasn't the first time she'd kissed Max Reardon, and it wouldn't be the last. She walked to the pool hall enjoying the utter peace downtown offered this time of night. Pine garland and red bows hanging from the turn-of-the-century style streetlights were dusted in white. Their soft light reflected off the dark windows of the businesses along Main Street.

Inside the pool hall, the lights blared brightly over the pool tables as many of the regular patrons enjoyed their favorite game of billiards.

"Hi, Ricky," Allyson said with enthusiasm as she approached him. "Is Max in his office? I brought his half of the money from the festival."

"No," he replied with an embarrassed smile, confirming her suspicion that he'd been the one to hang the mistletoe in the tent. "Max left early tonight. I think he went home."

"Okay, thanks. I think I'll stop by and surprise him," she said and handed him the cash-filled envelope. "Just put it in the safe. I'll let him know I gave it to you."

Deciding to not walk the short distance to Uncle Wally's cabin in heels, she went through the kitchen and out the rear door toward her car. It was parked in the back parking area in her private space. Uncle Wally lived on the other side of the city park, and it only took about five minutes to drive there.

A silver Mercedes sat parked in front of Uncle Wally's house. Allyson parked in the space ahead of it, wondering who it belonged to. A car that fancy stuck out like a sore thumb in this town.

People in West Loon Bay rarely knocked on their neighbors' doors. If the door was unlocked, they simply pushed it open, announced their arrival, and walked in. Max probably didn't know of that tradition, but he was about to be pleasantly surprised.

"Hey, Max," she shouted and shoved open his front door. "It's me, Allyson!"

The moment she walked in, she instinctively knew something was wrong. Max stood at his kitchen counter eating a sandwich, but when he saw her, his face paled—like he'd swallowed a tractor tire instead of a mouthful of bread. Guilt and panic were the only words to describe his stiff stance and the wild look in his eyes.

He dropped the rest of his sandwich into Sandy's dish. It had barely touched the bowl when Sandy stretched his tongue out and quietly wolfed down the food in two gulps. Patting the dog on the head he said to her, "What are you doing here?"

The abruptness of Max's question stopped her in her tracks. "I—Ricky said you'd left work early, so I dropped by to say hi. What's the matter?"

"I'm leaving," he countered abruptly as he walked toward her and pressed his hands upon her shoulders to guide her back out the door. "I'm sorry, but I can't stay. I have something urgent to do."

This wasn't the Max she knew. Not at all. Max wasn't pushy. Or rude. Something was wrong.

"May I come with you? I thought we could spend time together tonight. I mean, we both have the night off and—"

"*Max...*" a sultry voice slowly echoed behind him. "I'm getting bored. Come to bed."

He suddenly turned to stone, pivoting stiffly.

Allyson peered around him and saw a beautiful woman standing in the bedroom doorway, mid-fifties with dark, curly hair, ruby red lips, and sparkling diamonds adorning her ears and neck. Wearing nothing but a sheet draped across her long, sleek body, she stood like a goddess, leaning against the doorframe.

Sybil King.

Max drew in a shaky breath, struggling to control his anger. "I told you to get dressed!"

"But, darling… I *need* you."

For a moment, Allyson stood riveted in place absorbing the gravity and hurtful humiliation of what she'd accidentally interrupted.

Sybil and Max…?

Sybil leaned against the door, a sly smile curving her full red lips.

"She's right," Allyson said slowly, deliberately as she glanced from Max to the woman he'd swore to her was *long gone*. How could he kiss her at the festival and act like he cared about her when all along this…this wily, oversexed bimbo was lying naked in his bed? What kind of sleazy, egotistical game was he playing? Worse yet, did he really think that he could get away with something like this without it getting back to her? West Loon Bay was gossip central! She stepped back toward the door. "From what I can see, I think she needs you more than I do."

Max's eyes filled with confusion and fear as though he realized he'd put himself in a no-win situation. "Allyson don't leave. I know what it looks like, but I can explain. This isn't what you think it is."

She threw open the door, not in the mood for his excuses. "No, it's far worse."

His body filled the doorway as she fled down the steps to her car. "Allyson, wait! Please! Give me a chance to straighten this out. I didn't invite her, and I swear, I didn't sleep with her."

Ignoring his pleas, she jumped into her car and drove back to The Ramblin' Rose to barricade herself in her office and lick her wounds.

I should have known he was too good to be true, she thought to herself as she fought back tears. *He led me to believe he was one in a million when really, he's no better than my ex-boyfriend.*

She parked her car and went through the kitchen of The Ramblin' Rose keeping her head down to avoid attention. It didn't work.

"Allyson, what's wrong?" Grace asked, picking up immediately on her grave emotional state. "What happened?"

"It's—it's nothing," Allyson replied with a catch in her voice as she headed toward the office.

Grace grabbed her by the arm and steered her toward the bar. “Yes, it is. I’ve never seen you look so upset in my life. C’mon, you need a glass of wine to calm your nerves. Knowing how happy you were when you left here to be with him, this has to be about Max.”

Relenting, Allyson shrugged her jacket off and slipped onto a bar stool, tucking it onto her lap. Resting her elbows on the bar, she sipped a glass of Riesling and poured her heart out to her cousin.

“I don’t get it,” Grace said with a shrug. “That doesn’t sound like Max at all. I think you need to talk to him again and listen with an open mind to what he has to say, but for now, I want you to sit here and calm down. Take in the music and have something to eat. You need to be in a better frame of mind before you approach him.”

Allyson stared glumly into her wine glass. “After what I saw, I don’t care if I ever see him again.”

Chapter Twelve

Max waited until Sybil dressed, then assisted her with her fur coat and escorted her out to his car. No way would he allow her to drive. He drove to the back of the pool hall and parked in his reserved spot then ushered Sybil into the building, ignoring the surprised stares that followed him as he pushed Sybil into a booth and ordered a cup of coffee for her. Nothing fancy, just hot, black, and strong. He wanted her at least partially sober by the time Leo arrived to fetch her.

"Who's that, Boss?" Ricky asked warily as he stared at her.

"Trouble," Max replied and turned his back to the fur-clad woman in the booth. "Don't let her out of your sight. Her old man is on his way and should be here in a few minutes to take her home."

He gestured toward two men sitting at the far end of the bar, dressed in designer workout clothes and eating burger baskets. "Who is that?"

"Don't know," Ricky stated, "but they've been here all day, sipping Cokes and playing pool."

"What kind of hospitality is this, Max," Sybil grumbled and refused the steaming mug the server tried to set in front of her. "I want a drink!"

Max grabbed the coffee mug from Joy and placed it on the table in front of Sybil. "Sorry, but this is all you're going to get. I want you sober by the time Leo gets here."

Sybil pushed the coffee away and glared at him. "Drunk on a mere bottle of wine? Don't insult me."

He moved close to Ricky. "There might be trouble when her husband gets here. Be ready."

Ricky's eyes widened at the news as he peered past Max and stole a glance at Sybil. "Okay…"

* * *

Leo Lawrence strolled into the pool hall a few minutes later, a short man, well-dressed with the air of Napoleon, flanked by a pair of burly bodyguards. The dark-eyed, graying gentleman wore a long cashmere coat in charcoal gray with a matching Fedora. He carried a black walking cane with a silver embossed handle.

"Hello, Leo," Max said tersely and pointed to a booth in the corner where Sybil sat, her coffee untouched, scrolling her phone. She glanced at Leo, glared at him and pushed her phone aside. "Your *wife* is ready for you to take her home. Her Mercedes is parked in front of my house. Take that away, too."

Ignoring the fierce stare from his better half, Leo used his walking cane to point toward a table. His bodyguards pulled it to one side, placing one chair next to it. He removed his overcoat, handed it to one of the servers, and sat down. With a slight jerk of his head, he signaled to his suit-clad escorts. "Clear the place."

The pair immediately began bellowing at people to leave, including the staff, shoving everyone toward the front door. Anyone who put up a fuss got thrown out.

Ricky became agitated at seeing his customers get tossed around like punching bags, but Max laid a hand on his arm. "The guys can handle themselves. I need you to stay calm. Don't leave."

He approached Leo. "Look, there's no need for violence. This is between you and me. The truth is obvious so let's make this meeting short. I didn't invite Sybil here. She conned my whereabouts out of my mother and showed up on her own. I didn't get her drunk and I didn't lay a hand on her. Not tonight. Not ever. I wouldn't do that to you."

"He's a liar," Sybil said as she exchanged glances with the two men at the end of the bar. "He wanted to get even with you for ruining his reputation. He said if I didn't drive up here and spend the night with him, he'd kidnap me!"

Ricky stifled a laugh, managing to cover it by clearing his throat.

Max merely shook his head. "You know me better than that, Leo. I had five years and plenty of opportunities to carry on with her. Why would I suddenly start now? I don't know what her game is, but I'm not buying it." He paused, glancing from husband to wife. "What are you two *really* doing here?"

Sybil slid out of the booth as the two strangers from the bar flanked her protectively. "Trying to get to you first."

At Leo's signal, his bodyguards approached Sybil's escorts. Sybil's men pushed her behind them and closed ranks, facing off nose to nose with their challengers.

"It's time for you to leave!" one of Leo's men yelled into his opponent's face. He gave the man a push and suddenly fists were flying.

Max jumped into the fray. "Break it up, gentlemen! Time to leave. Come on. Let's go!"

Ricky stood at Max's side, dodging elbows and fists. "You heard what Max said! Take the fight outside!"

One of the men slammed Ricky in the face, knocking him against the wall. Max intervened and the fight began.

Chapter Thirteen

Allyson sat at the bar nursing her broken heart with a plate of warm mini-tacos and half-heartedly listening to the band play their last song of the set. "This is yummy, Grace," she said as she took another bite of the crispy, meat-filled shell. "What a great idea. I really like the sauce you poured over the taco meat. What is it?"

Grace laughed. "It's my secret! I don't want anyone to know because the taco plate is selling like crazy, and I don't want the pool hall cooks to copy my idea."

"Uh huh…" Allyson replied nodding. She took another bite. "Well, I'm definitely a fan."

Grace refilled her soda water. "Feel better now?"

Allyson sighed. "No, but I'm enjoying the tacos anyway."

A couple of regular patrons from the pool hall burst through the main entrance and headed straight for Allyson. One of the guys, a tall, lanky Norwegian with deep blue eyes, pulled his bill cap off as he approached her, his curly red hair flattened by the inside band. "Max is in trouble," he said breathlessly, sounding as though he'd run all the way. "He and Ricky are getting beat up!"

Shocked, Allyson dropped her taco and swung around. "What are you talking about, Del?"

"Some old guy came into the pool hall acting all Al Pacino-like with his paid muscle. They threw everybody out and locked the door. Two guys—no one knows who they are—refused to go and got into it with the old guy's gatekeepers. I don't know what the fight is about, but when one of them started pounding on Ricky, Max intervened."

"Hopefully, somebody called the cops," Allyson replied with a disinterested shrug. "It's Max's problem, not mine."

"I don't know. Max acted like it was a private matter." Del slipped his cap back on and pulled his gloves from his pockets. "I'm going back to find out what happened. I just wanted to let you know since he and you are…you know."

Since we are…what? she thought sadly. *Competitors? Friends to enemies?*

"All I got to say is," Del added, "Uncle Wally ain't gonna be happy about this when he comes back. His place is gettin' busted up."

What? She slid off the barstool. Poor Uncle Wally, sitting in a rehab facility trying to heal his knee, trusting his nephew to handle things in his absence while Max was literally bringing down the house. The old guy didn't deserve that.

"All right. I'll walk over there and see what's going on. If I find out things are out of control, I'm definitely calling 9-1-1 and I'll personally make sure Max replaces everything he ruined."

Del looked confused. "How are you going to get in? It's locked up tight."

"I know where there's a spare key," she said and grabbed her jacket from behind the bar.

"Just be careful," he warned. "You don't know who you're dealing with."

* * *

Allyson headed out the back door and walked across the blacktop that provided parking for employees and connected all the businesses along Main Street. At the rear entrance of the pool hall, she reached underneath the coach lantern above the door and pulled out a magnetic key box that contained a rusty key. It didn't take long to enter the warm kitchen, now deserted. She slipped the key into her jacket pocket and walked toward the angry voices. Sandy's barking rose above the fray.

The staccato clicks of her red spiked heels on the quarry tile announced her presence. Suddenly the shouting and scuffing sounds in the hall went completely silent. The moment she walked into the room, the crowd of spectators looking through the front windows erupted in an onslaught of shouting and waving to get her attention.

Sandy ran to her side and pressed against her legs. A sharp ridge of golden hair rose along his spine.

Ignoring the onlookers, Allyson glanced around and almost screamed from shock. "Max! You're hurt!"

Max stood facing off with two beefy men in dark suits. Blood flowed from his nose. His hair was a mess. His disheveled clothes were stained with blood, but he didn't seem to care. The moment their gazes met his eyes filled with worry. "Allyson, what are you doing here?"

Everyone else watched her curiously.

"Del told me there was a ruckus going on here and—"

Ricky sat curled on the floor, his left eye swelling and turning black like an overripe avocado. Her heart went out to him as she squatted beside him. "Oh, my gosh, Ricky! Are you okay?" Sandy sniffed his face and began to whine. "What happened to you?"

He gave her a sheepish grin. "I didn't get out of the way fast enough but don't worry about me. I'll be alright. How did you get in?"

"I have a key. I let myself in to make sure nothing happened to Uncle Wally's property," she said slowly as she stood up and took in the carnage, "but it looks like I'm too late."

"Allyson…this doesn't concern you," Max said through a swollen lip as he approached her and reached out to her. "Go back to The Ramblin' Rose and leave this to me. Please!"

No way, she thought to herself as she pushed his hand from her arm. *Not after seeing this…*

Wooden tables and chairs, broken beyond repair lay strewn about the room. Sparkly garland and ornaments lay on the floor in shreds, including the Christmas tree. The sight of so much senseless damage to both the men and the pool hall developed a rage inside her that burned like a wildfire. "What's going on, Max? Uncle Wally isn't going to be happy about this mess."

A gray-haired man sat at the only unbroken table in the place. She approached him and glared into his cold dark eyes. Sandy began to growl. "Are you responsible for this damage?"

One of the bodyguards moved toward her to intercept their discussion. Max jumped in front of him and the two began to shove each other until the old man waved them away. "Enough! I'll handle this."

He turned back to Allyson. "Lady, this is a private matter," he said gruffly and gestured toward the kitchen with his cane. "Go back to wherever you came from and mind your own business."

Surprised at the man's rudeness, she ignored his command. "Aren't you a little old for barroom brawls? Do you and your…" She glanced at his disheveled bodyguards, "*associates*…always barge in and act this way?"

The man's eyes narrowed as he stared past her. "I do when my livelihood is threatened."

Allyson turned to see the object of his focus and found Sybil King standing between her bodyguards—fully dressed in shiny black leggings and a sparkling red top, her ample cleavage in full view. Her gaze swept over Allyson with disdain as she folded her arms. "What's it to you?"

"The owner is a friend of mine," Allyson snapped. "And if I don't start getting some answers, you'll both be answering to the chief of police." She spun around, poking the old man in the chest with her finger. "Who, I might add is my uncle!"

Grabbing her hand, his grim stare softened into a slow smile as he intertwined his fingers with hers. "Look, there's no need for that, Missy. We're just having a discussion that got a little out of hand. Okay? I'm Leo Lawrence. And you are…?"

Allyson jerked her hand away. "I'm Allyson Cramer and I operate The Ramblin' Rose bar down the street. What do you want with Max?"

"It's none of your business," Sybil said acidly, cutting in. She nodded at the beefy, thirtyish man on her left. "Trent, get her out of here."

"Hey!" Max bellowed as the man grabbed Allyson by the arm. He swiftly moved toward them. "Let her go!"

Allyson jerked her arm away.

Leo stood, leaning on his cane. "Leave her alone! Let's get back to the matter at hand."

"Then we're going to be here all night because I'm not going to admit to something I didn't do," Max replied. "I never took advantage of your wife. When I worked for you, I looked up to you. I was *loyal* to you. You should apologize to *me*!"

"I'm aware of that," Leo said as he slowly returned to his chair, "and I concur. You're too smart and level-headed to fall for *her* tricks. That's why I want you to come back to work as my GM and I'm prepared to give you a substantial raise. If you would have spoken directly to me before you left, there wouldn't have been any need for you to quit."

Max's eyes widened in surprise at Leo's sudden announcement. "You—you what?"

"Don't listen to him!" Sybil shouted. "He's using you, Max! He simply wants you to take the job so his half of the company looks better on paper." Her eyes narrowed at Leo, telegraphing a hateful look. "He's made a deal with some corporation to sell his half of the company!"

They're both using him, Allyson thought cynically as she glanced from Leo to his wife. *Sybil found out Leo was selling out of their partnership, so she came on to Max, knowing that he'd walk away rather than betray the man he looked up to. His departure left a key position unfilled, throwing a wrench into Leo's negotiations.*

"And you're trying to stall it," Leo shouted. "But it's not going to work! I'm working with the buyers to make sure all my current employees will keep their jobs."

Allyson studied Max, trying to gauge his thoughts. He listened intently, but didn't give away his intentions.

Leo leaned forward in his chair resting his hands on the silver handle of his cane. "What do you say, Max? Are you in?"

"I…" As he spoke, Max looked deeply into Allyson's eyes, as though he expected her to speak up. When she stayed silent, he turned away and ran his hand through his hair. "No. I'm not interested."

Leo and Sybil began to argue again, hurling insults at each other. Sybil's bodyguards stepped in front of her and began to clash with Leo's men.

The crowd outside banged on the windows, erupting in shouts to open the door. Sandy began to bark again.

Allyson's phone suddenly rang. She pulled it from her coat pocket and glanced at the Caller ID. "Del," she said as she pressed the speakerphone. "What's up?"

“I can’t hold off these guys much longer,” Del said sounding breathless. “They wanna break the door down. Some of the guys are itchin’ to jump in and help Max turn the tables. Make it a fair fight.”

“No more fighting, Del! Tell them I said so! Call my uncle Bob. Tell him what’s going on. He’ll calm them down and send them home.”

“Somebody already called Chief Wyatt but I’m not sure I can get these hotheads to wait for the cops.”

If Max or I don’t do something to end this circus, somebody is going to get hurt, she thought worriedly as she hung up and shoved her phone into her pocket. She stepped in between the angry bodyguards, pressing her palms against their broad chests. “Gentlemen, you’re leaving. *Now*. Get your coats.”

One of Sybil’s men slapped her hand away and reached out to grab her. “Shut up! We don’t take orders from you!”

Before she could fend him off with a swift kick, Ricky sprang into action, while pulling her out of harm’s way. “Leave her alone!” he cried and circled his arm around her waist to protect her. “If you ever try to lay a hand on her again, you’ll have to go through me!”

Max rushed to Allyson’s side. “Are you okay?”

“I’m fine,” she replied quietly, “but we need to get everyone out of here before anyone else gets hurt.”

Max stepped forward pushing the men apart. “You heard what the lady said! Get out. Or would you rather get dragged out by that angry mob outside? Once they break that door down, I won’t try to stop them.”

Leo’s face darkened. “This is all your fault, Sybil! If you wouldn’t have made me look like a fool in front of my staff, it wouldn’t have come to this.”

A police siren wailed faintly in the distance.

“Let them out the back door,” Max said to Ricky. “Not because they deserve it, but because I don't want any more trouble." He turned to Leo. "We're done here."

Realizing Max meant what he said, Leo stood and slipped his arms into his coat. He shook his head. "You're making a mistake."

As the siren grew louder, Allyson held onto Sandy while Ricky and Max shepherded the group through the kitchen to the rear entrance. Max shut the door firmly behind them, locked it, and walked back into the hall.

"I'm sorry I stormed out on you, Max," Allyson said softly when he returned. "I should have believed you when you tried to tell me the truth. If I had, maybe none of this would have happened."

Max shook his head. "It's not your fault. I should have gone to Leo and explained what happened, but I didn't think it would do any good. He's been blaming others for his problems with Sybil for years. Maybe this confrontation will force him to either get a divorce or seek counseling. I don't really care. I don't want to deal with either of them ever again."

For his sake, she hoped he was right.

Chapter Fourteen

Ricky unlocked the front door giving way to a swarm of people filling the pool hall, but Max only had eyes for Allyson. "Are you okay? Did that jerk hurt you? When I saw him grab you, I went nuts—"

"No, I'm fine," she answered and handed him a couple of napkins to wipe the blood from his face. "What did you say to him to make him so angry in the first place?"

Max pulled out the chair Leo had used and eased himself into it with a groan. He and Ricky had put up a good fight, but two against four was twice as hard, especially when one came up behind him and sucker-punched him. He ended up with a smashed nose and a split lip, but his problems were paltry compared to the mess he had to deal with now.

"When I called him," he said as a sharp pain under his ribs made him wince. "I told him his wife was drunk, looking for trouble, and that she needed a ride home. He didn't appreciate the fact that Sybil led him on a long-distance wild goose chase."

Leo knew Sybil had been lying through her capped teeth, both times; once when she got caught kissing Max at the office and then getting caught sneaking up to West Loon Bay today, all to interfere with the sale of Leo's half of the spa. The weary, angry look in Leo's eyes tonight proved that he found his conniving wife's interference humiliating and repulsive. He probably wanted to divorce her in the worst way, but as Sybil had pointed out to Max back at the gym, Leo couldn't afford the legal nightmare, so he was stuck dealing with her. No wonder he wanted to sell out.

"Mr. Reardon," Chief Bob Wyatt's deep, gruff voice boomed as his tall, imposing form emerged from the crowd. "What have we here?" The police chief studied the scene, his brows raised at all the damage. "Care to tell me what happened?"

"Uncle Bob!" Allyson ran toward him and wrapped her arms around him. "Some men burst in here tonight and busted up the place. All the people here witnessed it. I didn't know the guys because they weren't local. They came from the Twin Cities, but they left just before you got here."

Chief Wyatt raised his hand to indicate silence as he stood with his hands on his hips, his ear cocked, listening to the dispatcher convey information to him. He acknowledged the information on his radio and turned his attention back to them. "One of the cars just got pulled over a couple of miles out of town for broken taillights and the State Trooper is asking for assistance. I'd better go and see what all the fuss is about, but I'll be back."

Gee, Max thought smiling to himself, *I wonder how those taillights got broken...*

After Chief Wyatt took his leave, Chris Peterson, the officer on duty tonight appeared, snapping photos of the damage and taking statements from the witnesses. Ricky and a few of the regulars stuck around to clean up the broken furniture and haul it out to the trash. One of the servers made matching ice packs for him and Ricky.

"Thanks for defending me against those thugs," Allyson said to Ricky as she wrapped her arms around him. "That was so sweet of you."

"Aw," Ricky replied, blushing. His shiner was going to be a real beauty by tomorrow. "I didn't want you to get hurt." He glanced at Max, a proud gleam lighting up his eyes.

Max nodded his approval and removed the ice pack from his lip. Setting it on the bar, he approached Allyson. “Hey,” he said softly. “Can we talk? In my office?”

She visibly stiffened at the grave tone in his voice. “All right.”

He led her into his office and shut the door. He couldn’t let her leave without telling her how much she meant to him. How much he wanted to patch things up between them.

“I’m sorry,” he said simply, “for all the trouble I put you through tonight because of me.”

Allyson leaned against his desk; her eyes were filled with sorrow. “That’s not necessary. It wasn’t your fault. You can’t control the actions of others.” She shrugged. “Especially *that* woman. She needs a twelve-step plan and a good shrink.”

He stared deeply into her eyes. “Look, this issue with Sybil has cast a dark cloud over us and I don’t want her to come between us anymore.”

“Max,” Allyson said sadly. “She isn’t what’s wrong with us.”

He gripped her shoulders. “I don’t understand. What are you saying?”

“You told me the day we met that you weren’t planning to stick around once your uncle returned. You’re a city kid. I’m a born-and-raised country girl. I serve drinks to farm boys. You’re a buff fitness trainer who is used to dealing with the elite. Beautiful, sophisticated women who are way above my pay grade.”

She pushed herself away from the desk and moved toward the door, putting distance between them. “I’ve been thinking about it all night. Sybil’s obsession with you isn’t a one-off, is it? It’s a fact of your professional life. What I’m trying to say, Max, is that you’ll never be happy here because the disparity between us is too great to survive a relationship. One day, you'll get homesick for the money and the glamour of your old life and then I'll lose you. Well, I'd rather lose you now before you have the power to shatter my heart."

His heart began to pound at the thought of losing her. "Allyson, I wouldn't do that to you, I swear! You're the best thing that's ever happened to me. Please, don't go."

"Goodbye, Max." She left his office, shutting the door behind her.

* * *

Friday, December 20th

Max spent the next few weeks refurbishing the pool hall with new furniture and decorations, touching up the scuffed walls, and training Ricky to take on more managerial responsibilities. In his spare time, he'd worked on his resume and applied online for a few jobs but so far, he hadn't come across anything that stood out to him. The desire he once had to start a new business had faded now, leaving him unsettled. However, he needed to stay busy to keep his mind off Allyson and the disastrous end to their short-lived relationship.

He thought that the passage of time and the prospect of getting a new job would lessen the blow, but it hadn't helped. Knowing that she was merely a block away drove him crazy. He wanted to walk down to The Ramblin' Rose and talk some sense into her. The only thing that kept him away was knowing that she'd probably reject him again.

He sat holed up in his office, staring at the wall. The morning had been quiet due to a slow-moving weather system that had dumped wet, sticky snow on the town overnight. Most people were home shoveling themselves out. It surprised him then when he heard a loud commotion in the pool hall. Opening the office door, he stared across the hall at a small mob of people at the front entrance. They separated and a slightly slimmer version of Uncle Wally emerged, pushing a slow-moving walker.

Max didn't know whether to be relieved that his job here had concluded or to panic because his uncle's return meant he was no longer needed and therefore free to return to his old life in Minneapolis. Sadly, the prospect of moving back to his empty condo held little appeal. He used to like coming home to a cold beer, his overstuffed sofa, and big screen TV after a long, appointment-filled day at the fitness center. Not anymore. He'd made so many friends at the pool hall that he enjoyed the daily camaraderie here in West Loon Bay.

Uncle Wally shuffled slowly through the large room soberly taking in the establishment's new look. He sat down at a table noting the cushioned seat of the metal chair and pushed his walker aside.

"Hey," Max said with the biggest "welcome home" smile he could muster. "It's good to see you again! You must be doing well to get back so soon. We didn't expect you until after Christmas. Did you drive yourself?"

Uncle Wally shook his head. "I can't drive yet. Rose brought me home."

Maddie appeared at the table with a joyful smile and filled their water glasses. "Do you want your usual lunch?"

Uncle Wally nodded his consent and lifted his shiny new water glass, staring at it. "The ice maker is working again?"

Max grinned. "Didn't take much," he said with a shrug. "I cleaned it out and replaced a couple of parts. I also unplugged a couple of drains and put in new soda lines in the beverage dispenser too."

Uncle Wally glanced around, a frown deepening his snowy-bearded face. "You painted and bought new furniture. How much did that set me back?"

"Not much," Max replied, stunned at his uncle's show of disappointment over all the work he'd put into cleaning and disinfecting this glorified petri dish. A few gallons of paint didn't cost much. Leo Lawrence had written a generous check to cover the new tables and chairs. "We needed it to increase our customer base."

Uncle Wally rested his beefy hands on his rounded stomach. "There was nothing wrong with the old stuff." He looked around again. "Where are all of my friends?"

"They come and go," Max said becoming wary of the interrogation. "A few got tossed out permanently. I don't tolerate any rough housing around here or disrespect to the servers."

Ricky walked up to the table and stuck out his hand to shake. "Hey, Uncle Wally! Glad you're back!"

"You've changed," Uncle Wally blurted. "You look older and taller like you've grown an inch or two."

No, Max thought. *He doesn't slump anymore from an inferiority complex. He's finally becoming the man he was destined to be.*

"Now that I'm back, things are going to return to normal," Uncle Wally announced gruffly. "Burgers, brats, and beer!"

Max went silent, taken aback by his uncle's emphatic announcement. It sounded like he'd just been fired.

Chapter Fifteen

Monday, December 23rd

Allyson stood behind the bar, slicing lemons when the back door opened, and Ashton appeared. She slipped out of her coat and walked through the kitchen into the bar.

Something about her cousin looked odd. Ashton wore jeans and her Ramblin' Rose T-shirt. Was that a coincidence or did it signal something else?

Grace emerged from the kitchen with a baffled look on her face, wiping her hands on a towel.

Allyson set down her knife. "Hi," she said cautiously to Ashton and then glanced at the large round clock on the wall. It was ten o'clock in the morning. "What are you doing here? Shouldn't you be at work?"

Ashton slid onto a barstool and pulled the elastic band from her long, silky brown hair. "I quit," she said quietly. "I want my job back."

Allyson and Grace both stared at her in astonishment.

"What?" Allyson and Grace burst out together.

Grace dropped her towel on the bar. "Why? What happened?"

"I can't stand working for Sawyer," Ashton spouted with a stubborn look on her face. "Get me this, get me that. Do this, do that. No cell phones while we're working. Go to the bathroom on your break!" She sniffed as though fighting back angry tears. "He has more rules than Dad used to enforce at home! All we do is argue now. I hate it. I'm not cut out to be his helper. I need to be my own boss."

Allyson tossed a coaster on the bar and then reached into the cooler, pulling out a frosty mug. "Is he okay with that?"

Ashton rubbed the moisture from her eyes with the backs of her hands. "Not really, but he can't stand the fighting either. He knows I'm not happy."

Allyson filled the mug with fizzy Coke from the soda gun. "Here," she said and pushed it toward her cousin along with a napkin to use as a Kleenex. "Drink this while we fill you in on the changes we've made while you were gone."

At this point, rejoicing that she'd come back at Sawyer's expense seemed inappropriate and unfeeling, but the excitement dancing in Grace's big brown eyes reflected Allyson's sentiment as well.

Ashton sipped her Coke, angling her head in curiosity. "What'd I miss?"

"We got the dishwasher fixed," Grace said proudly, "but the repairman said it's only a matter of time before it breaks down again or totally croaks. It's absolutely essential that we save for a new one."

"Between the booth on Main Street and the festival goers who came into the bar, we made a lot of money on Thanksgiving weekend," Allyson chimed in. "We paid all the bills, even the ones we were behind on, and actually had something left over. Business isn't great, but it has been better since then."

"Oh!" Grace squealed. "You need to try my new taco plate!" She ran into the kitchen to fix a plate for her sister.

The girls chatted while Ashton wolfed down her tacos, catching up on the latest gossip around town.

"Hanging out with you two is one of the things I've missed the most," Ashton said with a laugh as she licked her fingers. "Working with a crew of guys every day was like being on a desert island with a pair of fanatic sports fans. That's all they ever talked about!" She finished her Coke and set the empty mug on the bar. "How's Max, doing, Allyson? I heard about you two kissing under the mistletoe."

Her heart skipped a beat. "I haven't seen him for a while," Allyson replied, quickly downplaying the question. "He's super busy and so am I. And as for that kiss…" She shook her head with more enthusiasm than she'd intended. "It was nothing."

Ashton cast her a skeptical look. "That's not what I heard."

"Well, you heard wrong. There is nothing going on between Max Reardon and me. Ricky Palmer hung that mistletoe in the tent as a joke."

"I didn't know about that incident!" Ashton leaned against the bar and laughed. "I'm talking about you and Max at The Cove restaurant. That's where Ricky got the idea."

Embarrassed that Ashton had heard about their kiss at the resort, Allyson emptied the ice from Ashton's mug and plunged it into hot, soapy water in the bar sink to busy herself. "The Cove? How did he find out about that?"

"Didn't you recognize the photographer?" Ashton asked with a knowing grin. "That's Ricky's cousin. She tried to sell you a Christmas photo."

Oh, my gosh, Allyson thought miserably. *Everybody in town must be talking about us.*

Deep in her heart, she yearned to see Max again but knew the best thing for her was to steer clear of him until he went back home. Now that Uncle Wally had returned, it wouldn't be long.

At eleven o'clock, Ashton unlocked the front door and greeted someone enthusiastically.

Allyson looked up from double counting the money in her cash drawer to see Uncle Wally slowly enter the bar with his walker and make his way to the closest table. He looked thinner and older since the last time she saw him. The care on his face was unmistakable.

"Hey, there," she said and walked over to his table with a glass of ice water. "I heard you were back. It's good to see you! How are you?"

"Hungry," Uncle Wally barked as he half-sat, half-fell into his chair. "You still serve wild rice soup with warm lefsa and butter on Mondays? Doc says I gotta watch my cholesterol but not today. I've been craving your soup for weeks."

Grace gave him a big hug. "You bet. It's on the house!"

Uncle Wally waved the notion away. "I'll pay for it. My nephew brought in a lot of money while I was in rehab," he remarked dryly. "Not that I care. I wasn't hurtin' for cash in the first place."

Allyson and Ashton both sat down at the table to visit with him.

"Oh yeah?" Ashton asked. "I know he made a lot of changes. How do you like the pool hall's new look?"

Uncle Wally responded with a grim frown. "I hate it! There was nothing wrong with it before I left. Now it looks like one of those foo-foo coffee houses. He painted all the walls in different colors! He even bought new tables and chairs. Fancy-schmancy stuff. There was nothing wrong with the old ones!"

Obviously, Uncle Wally hadn't heard yet about the fight Max and Ricky got into with Leo Lawrence's bodyguards and Allyson decided that she didn't need to be the one to inform him. First, what went on at the pool hall was Max's responsibility. Second, Uncle Wally seemed to be overly agitated about Max's handling of the place as it was. No need to upset him further.

"Is he planning to leave soon?" she heard herself say, not realizing what she'd said until the words came out. Though it was for the best, the thought of never seeing him again filled her with sadness.

"I hope so," Uncle Wally replied crossly. "And when he does, he can take that ridiculous coffee contraption with him. He's driving me nuts. He cleaned out my cabin and now I can't find anything!"

Grace returned with his lunch and set it in front of him. His grumpiness melted away as he tucked his napkin under his chin and helped himself to a piece of warm lefsa, smearing a glob of fresh butter on it and rolling it up like a scroll.

Several new customers arrived and seated themselves, prompting Grace and Ashton to fetch their aprons and get to work. Allyson pushed her chair back and stood to go back to the bar, but Uncle Wally signaled for her to stay.

"I shouldn't complain. Max is a good kid and extremely smart when it comes to business," he went on, "but the boy's got some issues. Been moping around like the Grinch since I got home. Can't pay attention, can't smile, can't figure out what he wants to do with his life. Looks like I gotta figure it out for him." He pulled out his old-fashioned flip phone and speed-dialed someone. "Ricky," he said, "it's time."

Allyson squinted at him in confusion as he snapped the phone shut and shoved it back into his overalls. Something didn't feel right about that call. "It's time for what?"

Uncle Wally picked up his spoon and dipped it into his creamy wild rice soup. "My dear, I've decided to take the situation into my own hands. My nephew needs a little help in matters of the heart and so do you."

This time, Allyson did stand up, horrified as she gripped her hand on the edge of the table to steady her. "What do you mean by matters of the heart? What did you do?"

The front door suddenly burst open, and Max rushed in. "Uncle Wally, are you okay?" He skidded to a halt in front of the table, looking totally flummoxed that his uncle sat enjoying a hearty bowl of soup. “Ricky said your knee gave out and you fell…”

Uncle Wally looked up. “It was a lie, you idiot. An excuse to get you over here and you fell for it. Okay, done my part. Now, you two duke it out and get this lover’s spat between you settled.” He waved his hand toward the kitchen. “Go on. Git. Let me eat my lunch before it gets cold.”

Everyone in the bar stopped talking, curiously watching them.

Max looked into her eyes. Though he didn’t speak at first, the loneliness and desperation on his face spoke volumes. He placed his hand on her arm. “Let’s get out of here.”

* * *

Allyson grabbed her jacket and left with Max by the back door. Feeling extremely awkward, she jammed her hands into her pockets as they stood on the wide back steps.

“What did you drag me out here to talk about,” she said warily.

“To set the record straight, Allyson,” Max stated honestly. “I know it looks like my rushing over here to check on Uncle Wally was staged, but I didn’t put him up to that, I swear. He planned it all by himself. Well, him and Ricky.”

She frowned and folded her arms to keep the cold from seeping in under her coat. “What does he think he’s doing?”

“Isn’t it obvious?” Max let out a deep sigh and looked up at the cloudy sky.

“He said you have issues. That you’ve been moping around like the Grinch,” Allyson stated bluntly. “Why?”

He looked into her eyes. “You know why. I finally figure out what I want to do with my life and the person I want to do it with changes her mind about me.”

"But Max—"

He gripped her by the arms, pulling her to his chest as he drew her face close to his. "Look, I need to say this and get it off my chest. I'm in love with you, Allyson. I want to be with you and I'm not going to change my mind. Ever. I admit, I didn't come here to lose my heart. I used Uncle Wally's predicament to escape a bad situation. But that day we met, the moment I saw you, somehow, I just knew… It rattled me so badly I almost dropped the lattes." He closed his eyes and sighed as though the memory still affected him. "I can't stand the way things are broken between us. I can't live without *you*."

His confession shocked her so much she began to sway with dizziness. Gripping his shirt for support she leaned her forehead against his chest. "Oh, Max. I've been in love with you ever since you kissed me at the resort. I was so shaken by it that I thought my knees would collapse on the spot." She looked up. "No one has ever affected me like you did."

He slid his arms around her waist, holding her tightly. "Then why did you push me away when I tried to apologize to you at the pool hall?"

"Because…" she said as her voice began to shake, "I knew how you felt about small-town life. I told you the truth when I said that I was afraid you'd realize one day how much you were missing by giving up your career and then you'd leave me."

He curved his palm around the nape of her neck, fondling her ear with the pad of his thumb. "For the record, I have no career. Now that I've rejected Leo's offer, he'll never give me the reference I need to get another job like the one I left and frankly, I don't care. I just want to be with you. I want to build a life here—with you. Without you, nothing matters."

"Oh, Max." She slid her arms around his neck and kissed him, slowly and with purpose. The deep woodsy aroma of his aftershave filled her nostrils with his manly scent. She relaxed, leaning into the gentleness of his strong arms. "I just want to be with you, too, but I'm saddled with so many problems right now it's hard to visualize building a new life. Every week it's a headache trying to make ends meet. If The Ramblin' Rose isn't making a decent profit by the end of the year, we won't have any choice but to shut down."

Max pulled back and slid his fingers under her chin, tilting her face upward. He frowned at her like she was crazy. "You're kidding, right? If you made a few changes, this place could be a gold mine."

She laughed mirthlessly. "Yeah, fool's gold. No, seriously, Max, you pulled all our business away when you revamped the pool hall."

He laughed incredulously. "So what? We'll just pull it back."

"That would take a miracle," she argued, "and I don't have a magic wand."

"No, you have me," he said with a loving smile. "A perfectionist—like you. Together we'll reinvent The Ramblin' Rose and build it back to the hotspot it used to be."

She let out a defeated sigh. "Yeah, until the dishwasher breaks down again and we have to find the money to pay a repairman to fix it."

He answered with a wry chuckle. "What, like fixing it is hard? My uncle's dishwasher is a piece of junk. I've had to fix it three times. Don't worry about it. I'll take a look at yours this afternoon." Framing her face with his hands, he kissed her again. "Actually," he whispered, "I think we should spend a few hours after the lunch rush is over strategizing to get this place turned around by New Year's Eve."

She looked up at him as a rush of hope filled her heart for the first time in months. "I *could* use your help. Even with Ashton back on board, the extra help has been a relief to Grace and me, but we still have a long way to go to turn this place around. We've been so concerned about making ends meet that we didn't plan anything for New Year's Eve. Putting on a party would drain our account and if we didn't make the money back…"

"Great! Then we've got a clean slate to work with. We'll buy an ad in the local paper to let everyone know that we're throwing a big bash with lots of dinner specials, a DJ, and a bunch of mystery giveaways. If we can't find a DJ at this late date, we'll rent the equipment, and I'll do it myself."

Laughing with relief, Allyson locked her arms around his neck and hugged him, suddenly energized with enthusiasm—something she hadn't experienced in a long time. "Oh, Max! I can't wait to tell the girls that we might not have to close the bar. This is going to be so awesome."

"You're the one who's awesome," he said as he opened the door to go back inside. "We're going to be dynamic together."

Their future never looked brighter.

Epilogue

New Year's Eve

From behind the bar, Allyson smiled to herself as she took in the great job Grace and Ashton had done with the decorations for tonight's festivities. The Ramblin' Rose glowed with extra strings of bright, multi-colored Christmas lights strung around the room. In the dining area, a lit candle garnished each table along with a small centerpiece made of flocked pine sprigs, red berries and miniature ornaments.

On the corner stage, the decorated tree had been pushed back to make way for a local DJ who worked diligently, setting up his equipment for the evening's entertainment.

Ashton's husband, Sawyer, sat in a director's chair at the entrance, greeting everyone who entered. He and Lucy, his black Labrador mix, wore gray vests with "Security" printed on them. A string of blinking mini-lights lit up Lucy's breakaway collar.

Ashton stepped up to the service well and placed her tray on the counter. She wore a pair of black slacks covered with a long black chef's apron, and a long-sleeved white shirt with a sparkly red bowtie. Her glossy brown hair had been woven into a French braid, accented with tiny red velvet bows. "Two frostbite martinis and a glass of Chablis."

"How are you doing?" Allyson asked as she poured coconut

cream, Blue Curaçao and rum into a blender along with a handful of ice. "Are you and Sophie able to keep up?"

"Yeah," Ashton said as she glanced back at her tables. "The dining room has been steadily turning over since three o'clock and we've got reservations right up until the kitchen closes, but we've got a system going where we help each other out." She leaned forward. "We're getting good tips tonight. Especially on the 'Dinner for Two' special. Everybody loves the fancy holiday drinks we paired with the meals. How are you doing?"

Allyson wore a pair of red velvet leggings tonight, red flats, and a pearly white shirt for both ease and comfort. She wiped her hands on her red chef's apron and pulled a beer mug from under the counter, crammed with dollar bills. "So far, so good." She smiled. "Grace is going to be happy. She's the busiest of us all."

At the end of the night, Allyson and Ashton always pooled their tips together and split them three ways, giving Grace a share.

Ashton glanced around again. "Where is Max?"

Allyson stuffed the mug back under the bar and placed the cover on the blender. The machine whirred, turning the liquor into a creamy blue froth as she dipped the rims of two martini glasses into a dish of sugar, creating a "frosty" look. "I sent him down the basement with a list of liquor bottles to get for me before it gets *really* busy in here." She laughed. "I'm looking forward to our first time tending bar together."

Ashton smiled. "You really love him, don't you? Your face glows every time you talk about him."

Allyson turned off the blender and pulled off the top. "Does it show that easily?" She smiled, thinking about how the last few weeks with Max had become a dream come true. "I didn't like him the first time we met. I got spitting mad at Grace for accepting his luncheon invitation, but that day changed my life."

Ashton laughed. “Max can fix *anything*, and Sawyer can build anything. If Grace hooks up with a guy who can do wiring and plumbing, we’re set!”

They laughed but Allyson appreciated what an asset Max was turning out to be for the bar. He’d worked non-stop for a week, fixing broken chairs, replacing light bulbs and checking all their systems to make sure nothing went wrong tonight. They had a busy night ahead of them and it was only seven o’clock, but she’d never felt so energized before. So happy…

By eight o’clock, the DJ began playing to a full house. Allyson got so busy making drinks alongside Max that she paid no attention to anything else.

“JD on the rocks, a rum and coke and two Mics,” Ashton said as she wiped off her tray and set it on the counter. Then, in a surprise move, Ashton suddenly slipped behind the bar.

Allyson shot her a sideways glance as she worked, her hands flying faster than her thoughts. “Ash, what’s up?”

“Don’t look now,” Ashton murmured in a stage whisper, “but after I leave, check out the people at table number ten.”

Allyson’s hands stilled for a moment, wondering who that could be…Sybil King? Perhaps, Sybil, Leo and their *associates*?

Oh-oh, Allyson thought nervously. *What are they doing here?*

But when she finally sent Ashton on her way with a trayful of drinks and she looked across the room, the couple at table number ten didn’t resemble Sybil and Leo at all. Even so, they looked vaguely familiar…

She froze.

Oh. My. Gosh.

“What’s going on?” a deep, sexy voice whispered in her ear.

“You look upset.”

Standing so close that his shoulder touched hers, Max squinted, straining to see what had caught her attention. After a moment, he turned to her with a puzzled frown deepening his brow. “I don’t see anything unusual. What’s wrong?”

Allyson let out a tense sigh. “Not what, Max. Who…”

He blinked in confusion. “Who then? Your parents? A friend?”

“More like a mortal enemy,” Allyson replied slowly as she stared across the busy room. “See that couple in the corner? The blonde and the guy in the Bob Dylan sweatshirt?” She grabbed a couple of beer mugs off the bar and plunged them into hot, soapy water in the sink. “That’s Janeen Murphy and Finley Grange.” She turned to him. “My ex-business partner and my ex-boyfriend.”

Max burst out a sarcastic laugh. “What are they doing here? Did you invite them?”

“Of course not!” She grabbed the clean mugs and dunked them into the sink of plain water then set them upside down on the drainboard. “I haven’t seen them since they raided our business account and ran out of town, but knowing Janeen, she has a reason to swallow her pride and show up here. She never does anything unless it benefits *her*.”

After that, Allyson and Max were too busy to even talk, much less pay attention to Janeen and Finn. Allyson had her hands full making margaritas for a table of four in the dining room when she heard Ashton clearing her throat, a cue for her to look up.

Allyson lifted her gaze and nearly dropped the martini glass in her hand.

“Hi, honey,” Finn said in a low, sexy voice as though meeting up with her on New Year’s Eve in the Ramblin’ Rose was business as usual. Tall, thin and lanky with curly brown locks, time hadn’t changed him much except that now he had a mustache and longer hair.

Max stood pouring a shot, but his hands stilled, halting the process mid-air.

"Don't try to sweet talk me," she replied acidly to Finn. "I haven't been your *honey* since you snuck out of town in the middle of the night with my business partner—and our money. You've got a lot of nerve showing up here. Both of you. What do you want?"

He smiled glibly. "I don't have anything to do with your business partnership. That's between you and Janeen. Why don't you step away for a moment and stop by her table? She wants to talk to you."

"I have nothing to say to her," Allyson said as she poured out the margaritas into long-stemmed glasses rimmed with salt and placed a lime slice on the rim of each one. "Nothing that I can repeat here, anyway."

"Then let her do the talking," Finn coaxed. "She wants to apologize."

It's a little late for that... Allyson thought angrily.

"I'm too busy," she persisted and busied herself setting the glasses on Ashton's tray.

"Go on," Max whispered in her ear. "See what she has to say. We're caught up for now. I can handle the bar."

Letting out a taut sigh, Allyson wiped her hands on a bar towel and tossed it aside. She pulled the sash on her apron and slipped it over her head. "I'll be right back," she said as she tossed it on the back bar. "But if you hear screaming, you'd better rescue her before I pull out all of her bleached hair!"

The stares of curious patrons followed her as she made her way to a booth along the back wall where Janeen waited in a sparkly green designer dress, swirling a swizzle stick in her cranberry sangria. She'd grown her blonde hair long and wore it in wide-barreled curls. The tight line of her full, rose-colored lips indicated that she was nervous.

"Finn said you wanted to speak to me," Allyson said directly, forcing herself to keep her voice civil. She clasped her hands together in front of her to keep them still. Why would Janeen want to talk to her after all this time? And why do it publicly? She had something up her sleeve. Allyson had no idea what it was, but instinct warned her to be careful.

Janeen looked up, her patrician face paling as she glanced around before meeting Allyson's gaze. "I…I wanted to tell you how sorry I am for what…what I did to you." She glanced around again as though gauging the mood of the people watching her. "The money…leaving you to deal with bankruptcy court…and everything else."

Allyson stared at her, knowing they were being watched by nearly everyone in the bar by now. "By *everything else*, do you mean Finn?" She shrugged and dismissed the notion with a wave of her hand. "I was upset at the time, but I'm over it. He's more suited to you, anyway."

A cheat and a liar, just like you... she thought to herself. *You deserve each other.*

Janeen let out a sigh of relief. "Thank you. I'm so glad there are no hard feelings between us because—"

Allyson could feel it coming. The pitch. The girl wanted something from her. Something bad enough to risk public humiliation to get it… "What's the catch, Janeen? You didn't come here tonight and risk getting thrown out just to ask for forgiveness. I know you better than that. What do you want?"

Janeen suddenly dropped the penitent act and folded her arms, glaring at Allyson. "Finn and I are getting married next month in town so we don't want this…this issue between you and me hanging over our wedding like a dark cloud."

"What does your wedding have to do with me," Allyson asked, puzzled. "I'm sure I'm not on the guest list so why does it matter whether we kiss and make up or not?"

Janeen defiantly lifted her chin. “A lot of people in town are sympathetic towards you and it’s going to hurt the attendance to our wedding unless you and I settle this once and for all.”

Allyson almost burst out laughing at the thought. Leave it to Janeen to make it sound like she was ruining the wedding of her exes. Sympathy was the last thing Allyson needed. Or a public scene. What she truly could use right now was to get ten grand of their company’s money back to pay Sawyer the money she owed him, but she knew that would never happen.

Suddenly, Max’s strong arm encircled her waist, pulling her into the crook of his arm. “Allyson doesn’t harbor any hard feelings against you,” Max said to Janeen. He smiled at Allyson. “Do you, babe?”

“What? I…I guess not,” Allyson replied slowly, wondering why he’d decided to intervene. “I mean, well—”

“What she means is that we’d like to congratulate you on your engagement,” he said and gazed at Allyson with a slow, sexy smile. “Right, babe?”

Janeen’s blue-eyed gaze swept across Max’s sculpted chest and tall frame, her expression indicating she was flummoxed by his unexpected appearance. She frowned. “Who are you?”

“I’m Max Reardon, Allyson’s new business partner and the love of her life,” Max replied with a disarming smile as he extended his hand. “It’s nice to meet you.”

He turned to Finn and extended his hand again. “I don’t believe we’ve met before,” he said in a measured tone. “Are you in town simply for the holidays or are you looking to get a place here?”

Finn shook hands, shrinking back at the pressure in Max’s handshake. “Ah…we haven’t decided yet.”

“We’d better get back to work,” Max said quickly and grabbed Allyson’s hand. “Ashton’s tending bar in our place. Enjoy your evening."

"No hard feelings? *Babe?* What was that all about," she asked him as they maneuvered their way through the crowd. "You realize who that is, don't you?"

"Of course, I do." He pulled her behind the bar and slid his arms around her. "Don't you see what they just did? This whole forgiveness business is just an act to get you to let them off the hook. They think they've *won*."

Allyson gazed at him curiously. "Haven't they?"

Max chucked and whispered in her ear. "Are you kidding? You won a long time ago because you didn't allow their actions to set you back. You got together with your cousins and reinvented yourself. It hasn't been easy, but if the reception we're getting here tonight is any indication of the future, you're going to be just fine. Those two, on the other hand, have nothing to show for their lives in this town but bad reputations."

"And I've got you," she said sliding her palms up his chest. "Forever."

"Forever," he murmured and kissed her earlobe. "Hey, I've got a little something for *you*." He reached under the bar and pulled out a flat package wrapped in gold foil paper with matching ribbon and a huge bow.

She gasped in surprise as he placed the gift into her hands. "What is it?"

Max grinned. "Open it and find out."

Allyson carefully pulled off the ribbon and the bow then tore the paper off. "Oh, my gosh!" she said with a squeal. "You went back there and got this? For me?"

Max's eyes widened with uncertainty. "Do you like it?"

She laughed as she stared at the picture of her and Max kissing under the mistletoe at Peterson's Resort. "I love it!"

"Happy New Year, my love," he said cheerfully. "With many more to come." He slid his arms around her as she leaned into his embrace, her heart bursting with happiness. Her future was bright, filled with love, laughter, and endless possibilities. Tonight was only the beginning.

The End

A Note from Denise

Thank you so much for reading ***Mistletoe and Wine***. If you enjoyed this story, please take a moment to post a rating or short review on Amazon. Thank you! Ratings and/or reviews help me to reach more people who love to read sweet romance.

To be notified when a new book is available, be sure to follow me on Amazon at:

https://www.amazon.com/author/denisedevine

Passionate about sweet romance?

Want to be part of a fun group?

Visit us on Facebook at:

https://www.facebook.com/groups/HEAstories/

About Denise…

Denise Devine is a USA Today bestselling author who has had a passion for books since the second grade when she discovered Little House on the Prairie by Laura Ingalls Wilder. She wrote her first book, a mystery, at age thirteen and has been writing ever since. She loves all animals, especially dogs, cats, and horses, and they often find their way into her books.

She has written twenty-two books, including books in the Beach Brides series, Moonshine Madness series, and West Loon Bay series. Her books have hit the Top 100 Bestseller list on Amazon, and she has been listed on Amazon's Top 100 Authors.

If you'd like to know more about her, visit her website at:

https://www.deniseannettedevine.com

Have you read the West Loon Bay Series?

Welcome to West Loon Bay, Minnesota – A small tourist town poised on the shores of Lake Tremolo where the people are friendly and hard-working and there's never a dull moment in this close-knit community of second and third-generation Scandinavians. But everyone harbors secrets…

This small-town contemporary romance series is on Kindle and Kindle Unlimited.

https://www.amazon.com/author/denisedevine

Also in print and audiobook at your favorite retailer.

More Books by Denise Devine

Christmas Stories

Merry Christmas, Darling

A Christmas to Remember

A Merry Little Christmas

~*~

A Very Merry Christmas (Hawaiian Holiday Series)

~*~

Romance Books

The Encore Bride

Lisa – Beach Brides Series

Ava – Perfect Match Series

Della – Enchanted Island Series

~*~

Moonshine Madness Series – Historical Suspense

The Bootlegger's Wife – Book 1

Guarding the Bootlegger's Widow – Book 2

The Bootlegger's Legacy – Book 3

~*~

Charlotte Van Elsberg Mystery Series

The Nightingale Detective Agency – Book 1 - ***Coming Soon!***

~*~

West Loon Bay Series – Small Town Romance

Small Town Girl – Book 1

Brown-Eyed Girl – Book 2

Country Girl – ***Coming Soon!***

~*~

Christmas in West Loon Bay – Small Town Romance Series

Once Upon a Christmas

Mistletoe and Wine

~*~

Cozy Mystery

Dark Fortune - Fortunes, Love & Fate Series

Unfinished Business

~ Girl Friday Cozy Series ~

Shot in the Dark – Book 1

The Accidental Detective – Book 2 – ***Coming Soon!***

~*~

Forever Yours Series – Inspirational Romance

Always is Not Forever- Book 1

This Time Forever - Book 2

~*~

Other Books

Hot Shot – a humorous novella

Romance and Mystery Under the Northern Lights –short stories

Northern Intrigue – anthology of mystery stories

Boxed Sets

Merry & Bright – A collection of Denise's Christmas stories

Unforgettable Christmas Wonders

Unforgettable and Absolutely Fabulous Christmas Cheer

Reclaiming Me – Women's Fiction

~*~

~*~

Want more? Read the first chapter of my novels and get my complete book list at: **deniseannette.blogspot.com**

Audiobooks Galore!

Do you like audiobooks? Many of my books are available in audio!

Narrated by Lorana L. Hoopes

Check out my website for links to each audiobook.

Monthly sales!

www.deniseannettedevine.com/

www.ingramcontent.com/pod-product-compliance
Lightning Source LLC
LaVergne TN
LVHW010103110826
845155LV00028B/457

* 9 7 8 1 9 4 3 1 2 4 4 9 7 *